# Applause for *Dreaming Big*

"Knowing a little about 'dreaming big,' I have never seen such an organized approach to following your heart-and your Life Dream. *Dreaming Big* can help lift individuals and organizations out of mediocrity."

—Rich Devos
Co-Founder, Alticor & Owner, NBA Orlando Magic

—

"In our world today, society seriously needs a movement of dreamers. Biehl and Swets will surely help you find and implement your dream. I think this book is going to be very helpful to many, many people."

—Max De Pree
Former CEO of Herman Miller Corporation

—

"My father had a big dream . . . Holiday Inns. He was able to see his dream come true of a worldwide chain of hotels serving the public. Your dreams are uniquely your own. This book will help you realize that you, too, were 'made' for *Dreaming Big*!"

—C. Kemmons Wilson, Jr.
Principal, Kemmons Wilson Companies

—

"Bobb Biehl and Paul Swets can really write and engage the heart, the mind and the soul. Your future will be impacted by this important new book."

—Pat Williams
Senior Vice President, Orlando Magic

—

"Dream a big dream! Now, grab a pen and paper and Bobb Biehl and Paul Swets will walk you through a life-altering process in their energizing and inspiring book, *Dreaming Big*—a must-read for those ready to shift their 'inner-drive' into gear."

—Dan T.cathy
President and Chief Operating Officer, Chick-Fil-A, Inc.

"Reading *Dreaming Big* caused me to realize that I was the one holding back my own life dream. I highly recommend this book to everyone because for the small business owner, it will open up the possibility to dream big, really big, and keep that excitement alive. For the corporate executive, it will help you see how to hire the best talent and keep them at the peak of their capabilities by infecting them with their dream. For leaders everywhere, you will understand better why your people burn out, leave for greener pastures, or just muddle through-and how to turn them into eager, excited, top performers. *Dreaming Big* is a must read for anyone who wants to make a difference!"

—Brett Easley
Vice President, AutoZone, Inc.

"What a terrific book! I was planning to just skim through *Dreaming Big*, but found myself paying close attention to the wisdom on every page. It's a blueprint for a successful business and a successful life."

—Bob Burg
author of *Endless Referrals*

# Reader's Testimonials

"Extremely helpful! When I read *Dreaming Big,* I was re-evaluating my life and realized that I no longer had a dream. This book helped me define my dream, guided my actions to accomplish that dream, and kept me focused on the numerous possibilities for the second half of my life."

—Sarah R. Haizlip
Financial Planner, Summit Assets

"As children we are often asked, 'What do you want to be when you grow up?' As adults we should continue to ask ourselves similar questions: 'Where do you want to be in five years? In 10 years?' 'What would you do if you had adequate resources?' 'What would you do with your life if you didn't have to worry about a paycheck?' *Dreaming Big* prods readers to ask questions that energize them. It nudges readers into thinking about what is possible. And it frees readers to strive for those things that only the heart of a child would dare envision."

—Bevalee Pray, Ph.D.
Director of Graduate Programs in Business
Christian Brothers University

"I was raised to think that being a dreamer was kind of a shady thing. Now I understand that I was designed to dream, to joyfully pursue my dream, and to inspire dreams in others. For two decades I've had a dream of equipping the next generation of leaders. To that end, the step-by-step process in *Dreaming Big* has helped me clarify my life dream and learn how to get others to take my dream seriously. I've learned how to be a dream-releaser, not just a dreamer."

—Jeff Myers, Ph.D.
Founder, Passing the Baton International, Inc.

"What a great read! *Dreaming Big* will help many people capture and define their dreams. The book kept me interested. As someone who is still attempting to define my dreams, I will definitely use this book to achieve my goals. *Dreaming Big* is going to be a huge success."

—MAX PAINTER
DIRECTOR OF MARKETING
MEDTRONIC SPINE AND BIOLOGICS

"In *Dreaming Big*, Bobb Biehl and Paul Swets have touched on the heart of what it takes to lead a fulfilled life. They offer a clear prescription for how to achieve a rich and balanced life through finding avenues to be, to do, to have, and to help others. The book is especially helpful for those who must achieve their dreams through others, with its strategies for energizing a team and moving it toward the achievement of worthwhile goals and dreams."

—WILLIAM O. DWYER, PH.D.
PROFESSOR OF INDUSTRIAL PSYCHOLOGY
UNIVERSITY OF MEMPHIS

I was inspired by the practical steps offered in *Dreaming Big* to think through my life goals and to focus on a dream that is big but also manageable.

—RON MAN, INTERNATIONAL MUSICIAN

"Working with the BE, DO, HAVE, HELP CHART has caused me to see connections in my dreams and plans for the future that I had not seen before. I am very enthusiastic about the new insights this book has provided. You really have to read *Dreaming Big!*"

—MARIAM AYAD, PH.D.
PROFESSOR OF EGYPTOLOGY
UNIVERSITY OF MEMPHIS

# Dreaming
# BIG

You wonder . . .
*"Is it ok for me to dream? Is there any hope for my dream?"*

*Dreaming Big*
is dedicated to you.

# Dreaming
# BIG

Energizing Yourself and Your Team
With a Crystal Clear Life Dream

**Bobb Biehl & Paul Swets**

AYLEN
PUBLISHING

COLORADO SPRINGS • LONDON • HYDERABAD

Authentic Publishing
We welcome your questions and comments.

USA    1820 Jet Stream Drive, Colorado Springs, CO 80921  www.authenticbooks.com
UK     9 Holdom Avenue, Bletchley, Milton Keynes, Bucks, MK1 1QR
       www.authenticmedia.co.uk
India   Logos Bhavan, Medchal Road, Jeedimetla Village, Secunderabad 500 055, A.P.

Dreaming Big
Hardback                          Paperback
ISBN-13: 978-1-934068-30-4        ISBN-13: 978-1-934068-36-6
ISBN-10: 1-934068-30-6            ISBN-10: 1-934068-36-5

10 09 08 07 / 6 5 4 3 2 1

Published in 2007 by Authentic

Cover design: Walker + Associates · Memphis, TN · 901-522-1100
Interior design: Amy Huber
Editorial team: Amy Huber, KJ Larson

Printed in the United States of America

# CONTENTS

INTRODUCTION .................................................................... xi

**STEP 1**: *Discovering Your Dream*

Day 1   Creating Your Future.................................................3
Day 2   Beginning the Adventure...........................................7
Day 3   Shaping Your Dreams to Fit You.............................13
Day 4   Sharpening the Focus of Your Priorities.................18
Day 5   Tapping Into Your Natural Energy..........................23
Day 6   Asking Fog-Cutting Questions ...............................28
Day 7   Putting Together Your Life Dream...........................31

**STEP 2**: *Refining Your Dream*

Day 8   Choosing Your Direction Wisely.............................41
Day 9   Rethinking Your Life Work Based on Your
          "Life Dream".............................................................47
Day 10  Funding Your Dreams..............................................53
Day 11  Developing a Strategic Plan.....................................57
Day 12  Turning Dream Energy into Results ........................61
Day 13  Balancing Your Life .................................................67
Day 14  Stretching Beyond Childhood Labels .....................75

**STEP 3**: *Living Your Dream*

Day 15  Trusting Your Own Judgment...................................83
Day 16  Protecting Your Dreams...........................................92
Day 17  Overcoming Dismissal, Divorce, or Despair...........98
Day 18  Facing Unexpected Realities ..................................103
Day 19  Dreaming Breakout Dreams ..................................107
Day 20  Enjoying What Matters Most..................................113
Day 21  Mentoring the Next Generation .............................118

**STEP 4**: *Teaching Your Team to Dream*

Day 22  Demonstrating Leadership ..................................... 125
Day 23  Recruiting a Dream Team...................................... 130
Day 24  Asking Dream-Sparking Questions..................... 136
Day 25  Building a Team on Core Values......................... 141
Day 26  Helping Your Team See the Big Picture .............. 146
Day 27  Equipping Your Team to Overcome Failure........ 154
Day 28  Creating Competitive Advantage......................... 161

**STEP 5**: *Encouraging Your Team*

Day 29  Listening................................................................ 171
Day 30  Building ................................................................. 177
Day 31  Winning ................................................................. 184

Notes ...................................................................... 191
Acknowledgments ................................................. 195
Additional Resources ............................................ 196
Quick Wisdom.Com ............................................. 205
Bobb Biehl Speaking Topics ................................. 207

A *Dreaming Big* Tool Kit is available as a free download from
www.Aylen.com/dreamingbig.

# INTRODUCTION ➤ Wake Up and Dream

*If a man wants his dreams to come true, he must first wake up.*
*—Indian Proverb*

## When you examine your life, do you like where you're headed?

Since you've picked up *Dreaming Big*, perhaps you want a vision of your future that energizes you, gives meaning to everything you do, and enhances your relationships with everyone you meet. Perhaps you've seen this sort of life in enough people that you know it's possible and you want it too.

In *Dreaming Big*, Paul Swets and I invite you to discover, refine, and live your dreams—with your eyes wide open. We invite you to dig to the roots of your passions, to weed out what isn't productive, to water what brings you real happiness, and to enjoy the fruit of your labor.

Although the book is divided into 31 days, we know that "day" for one person may mean 15 minutes. Another may want to take a week for a section we call a day. Take your time. We do not want to overwhelm you . . . we want to inspire you. Among a number of dreams that you will identify this month, we anticipate that in the next 31 days you will discover one big Life Dream—a mental picture of the difference you want your life to make before you die.

Can you imagine how inspiring a Life Dream could be for you? Paul and I know the power of a Life Dream is nothing short of amazing. When your Life Dream is crystal clear, you can

- Express your dream in thirty seconds or less,
- Move on from where you are to where you want to be,
- Energize yourself for the rest of your life.

When you pursue your Life Dream, you will attract people who want to learn to do the same. They may even become part of a team of people you influence. That's why we have included a section on teaching your team about "Dreaming Big."

Just who are these teammates? At first your team may be your close family and friends. Then it might be several business associates or an organization of hundreds, perhaps thousands, depending on your Life Dream.

> **DREAMING BIG**
>
> *Everything I do from the time that I wake up until I go to sleep is connected with my dream.*
>
> *–David Genn*

*Dreaming Big* provides you a way to sort through the dreams you already have and build on their foundation. It gives you fifteen to thirty minutes of valuable insights for each day. In a month's time you will have transferable concepts that we believe will be worth many times the price of this book.

To make the best use of *Dreaming Big* concepts, remember the old adage:

I read $\longrightarrow$ I forget
I visualize $\longrightarrow$ I remember
I do $\longrightarrow$ I understand
I teach $\longrightarrow$ I master

You will find charts and illustrations to help you *visualize* your dream unfolding. Heart Probes at the end of each chapter enable you to *do* something with your ideas—think them through, write them down, act on them. *Teaching* others what you have learned will help you master these concepts, have more fun, and inspire others.

*Dreaming Big* is designed to make it possible for you to pursue two objectives:

- Energize yourself with your own Life Dream,
- Teach your team how to do the same.

We expect you will find dreaming big one of the most rewarding experiences of your life.


Bobb Biehl and Paul Swets


*"One can never consent to creep*
*when one feels an impulse to soar."*

Helen Keller

# STEP 1 ➤ Discovering Your Dream

*Look, and you will find it—what is unsought will go undetected.*
*–Sophocles*

Although you have dreams that are important to you, there may be one over-arching dream that has gone undetected. Look for it and you will discover it.

# Day 1

# Creating Your
## **Future**

*There is nothing like a dream to create the future.*
*—Victor Hugo*

## Overview

- *What Do I Want?*
- *Why Do I Want It?*
- *How Can I Achieve It?*

## Dreaming big energizes you to create your future.

Almost everyone dreams in their youth. They have not been programmed with negative messages. They are not discouraged by past failures or overwhelmed with work or burdened by other people's expectations. They are free to dream. They are excited about life.

Perhaps you catch glimpses of that "fired up life" now and then, but the actual attainment and maintenance of such peaks seems elusive. You may wonder if the process of pursuing dreams will benefit you.

In *Dreaming Big,* we map a path that has worked for many people. It will work for you. You can dream again. You can be guided through the fog and around the obstacles to your dreams. You can be encouraged to envision the future you truly want and helped to make it clear and compelling.

# What Do I Want?

When you search your heart, what do you want in life? Let your mind go. As you formulate answers, make a list of everything that comes to mind. If you need stimulators, check any of the following that might apply to you:

- Buy a new car or house
- Get out of debt
- Pursue a college degree or a profession
- Get married
- Start a family
- Enable my spouse to be home with the children
- Travel the world with my best friend
- Gain more control of my life
- Build affirming relationships with friends and business associates
- Be my own boss
- Own a profitable business
- Achieve financial independence
- Live free from personal, financial, and vocational worry
- Enjoy work that uses my greatest strengths
- Take quarterly vacations with my family
- Find peace and purpose in my everyday life
- Make a difference in others' lives
- Make a million and give away 50% of it.
- Change the world, one person at a time
- _____

**DREAMING BIG**

*I want to be able to help my parents out in their later years.*

*–Judith Scott*

What is important in *your* life? Don't worry about trying to meet someone else's expectations. Jot down your ideas in the margins of this book or in a journal. You may also download your *Dreaming Big Tool Kit,* a free collection of the questions, charts, and Heart Probes from www.Aylen.com/dreamingbig. As you reflect on your dreams, you will realize that some are on target and some will be far from your true center. We will coach you how to refine your list later on; so for now let your ideas flow.

## Why Do I Want It?

What motivates you to pursue your dreams? What difference will they make in your life or the lives of others? How will you feel? Will you smile more? Ok, why? Jot down *why* your dreams are important to you.

_____

_____

_____

You may not be able to answer that question just now. That's ok. But we will come back to it because, as psychotherapist Victor Frankl was fond of quoting, "The one who knows *why* can bear with almost any *how*." [1] Frankl discovered the power of this principle when he was in a concentration camp during the Second World War. He observed that even though the prisoners were treated the same, some survived while others did not. After interviewing the survivors, he learned that they endured the hardships because they had a "why," a reason to survive—a loving family, a sense of responsibility for others beyond themselves, a task they believed they were called to achieve.

David Genn knew why his dream was important to him. As executive director of AWANA International, an organization that works with more than a million children every week worldwide, the "why" compelled him to pursue a big dream.

One day I asked David, "Do you remember the day your dream for AWANA became clear to you, and do you remember what the results were?" David got excited just describing the beginning of his dream: "It was like the world exploded into color. I didn't know whether to laugh or cry or yell or run. I knew exactly what direction this organization should go."

"Whenever I make any bit of progress toward the dream, it's

a thrill. It's shooting a game-winning shot from mid-court as the buzzer goes off. Every day something happens and I say, "Yeah, one more step!" No matter what the increment of change, it's another charge to the battery. I have never gone through a twenty-four-hour period that the dream was not realized in some sort of incremental form. Never!"

## How Can I Achieve It?

What's the *next step* that will bring you closer to your dreams? Here are some actions to consider:
- Give yourself freedom to explore dreaming big
- Choose to eliminate procrastination and read this book
- Think creatively about you life and future
- Respond to the discovery questions and Heart Probes in each chapter
- Be patient with the process of gaining clarity about your dreams.

In the days ahead, we will help you take steps that will move you toward discovering your Life Dream by Day 7. But right now, use the *Heart Probe* that follows to discover the dreams in your own heart.

As you answer the following questions, remember: *dreaming big is a process*. Own it. Be patient with it. You have to get inside your heart. Go there. Trust your vision of what really is important in life. You were put on earth to fulfill a particular purpose. Look for it and you will discover it.

---

### *Heart Probe*

1. As I review the dreams in the *What Do I Want?* Section, p.4, what dreams are especially important?

2. How would I feel if I achieved any of these dreams?

3. Am I committed to taking the steps necessary to create my future? ____YES ____NO

---

# Day 2

# Beginning the
# **Adventure**

*Whatever you can do or dream, begin it.*
*Boldness has genius, power, and magic in it. Begin it now.*
*–Goethe*

## Overview

- *Discouragement*
- *Discovery*
- *Persistence*
- *Hope*
- *Discipline*

## Your adventure of dreaming big begins with taking the first step.

As a toddler, your very first steps brought joy to your parents. Even though you fell repeatedly, you got up and tried again. Gradually you made progress, gained confidence, and experienced the thrill of walking, climbing, running. Your life was full of adventure. And once the joy of adventure took hold of you, you were in for a wild ride.

Dreaming big is an adventure. It's a wild ride full of risk, even joy. Joy comes in the anticipation of success. But the process is not always clear or easy or organized. You may fall down and get bumped and bruised in the process. Yet dreaming big meets a deep human need for discovery, for excitement, for fulfillment.

In this chapter, you will discover five signposts that mark a journey of adventure. Let each signpost embolden you not only to dream fresh dreams, but to persist in the process. Then you will know the genius, power, and magic of dreaming big.

## Discouragement

The first indicator that you need to dream big is discouragement. For eleven years of my life, I had a dream that was so beautiful and so clear that I never lost energy in pursuing it. Every morning I woke up raring to go. I worked long hours, but I rarely got tired. I worked nights and weekends occasionally, and I never resented it because I had a dream.

When I was forty-three, two close friends approached me and suggested that my dream was unrealistic. I accepted what they said and let them steal my dream. For five years I didn't have a dream. As a result, I had very little natural energy. I lived on Diet Coke and worked mostly from discipline energy. My heart was heavy, my life dull, and my work was all drudgery and discipline.

One day I met with a man named Higgins Bailey to explore the possibility of working together. Unlike me, Higgins had lots of energy. About noon, Higgins asked, "Bobb, are you sad?" My immediate reply was, "Yes, I am." He asked, "Well, why are you sad?" To my surprise, I answered just as quickly, "Because I have no dream." Intuitively I understood that I needed a dream, although consciously I hadn't processed my situation to the point that I realized that a dream was the missing piece. At the end of the day, Higgins said, "Bobb, find a dream and then get back to me."

## Discovery

My discouragement prepared me for discovery. I was speaking at a conference of about 1,500 people with Angelo D'Amico at Hilton Head Island. One of the other speakers was Ron Hale, a man who has made millions in his business. He spoke about what makes a person successful. That night I decided to listen with "elephant ears" for the deeper meaning behind his words. I asked, "What is he really saying?"

Ron's first few sentences almost blasted me into the next room. He said, "Let me tell you what it takes to be successful in life. Number one, *you have to have a dream*. Number two, *you have to have a positive attitude*. Number three, *you have to have the right vehicle* to see that dream become real."

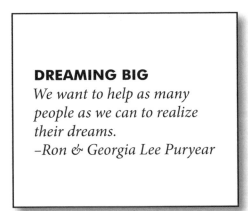

**DREAMING BIG**

*We want to help as many people as we can to realize their dreams.*

*–Ron & Georgia Lee Puryear*

Between "you have to have a dream" and "you have to have a positive attitude," my mind yelled, "Yes! This is why I'm here. This is what Higgins told me. This is what I used to have. When did I lose it? How can I get it back? Do I start with the old dream? Do I start with a new dream? Or do I start over?" All of these questions flashed in my mind the minute Ron said, "You have to have a dream." I knew he was right. That conviction led me to persist in searching for my dream until I found it.

## Persistence

Persistence also marked Paul's path in the pursuit of one of his big dreams. When he earned his doctoral degree in rhetoric from the University of Michigan, he began to dream of putting the insights he gained from his research into a practical format. He believed that increased communication skills could help couples build stronger marriages, and business associates build stronger organizations.

Twenty-five years ago, Paul acted on his dream. After work and when the children were in bed, he wrote on a legal pad from nine to midnight. For five years he wrote about principles he knew could make a difference and then sent off the manuscript . . . only to receive one rejection after another. Still energized by his dream, he kept on writing, polishing, knocking on doors.

Finally Prentice Hall cracked the door and Simon & Schuster opened it wide. Now, after more than twenty printings and over 100,000 copies sold, *The Art of Talking so that People Will Listen* keeps on helping people communicate with family, friends, and business associates. Paul knows that persistence is part of dreaming big.

## Hope

For us, persistence was fueled by hope. Hope can do the same for you. You can discover the energizing power of your dreams, even if the rejections and routines of life have all but choked them. Yes, tragedies do occur. In the course of life there is "a time to weep and a time to laugh, a time to mourn and a time to dance."[1]

It's no use putting on a "happy face" when it's time to mourn. Yet, if sorrow plagues your steps, if a marriage or family relationship has broken, if a career dream has failed, you must not give in to despair.

> *If you lose hope, somehow you lose the vitality that keeps life moving, you lose that courage to be, that quality that helps you go on in spite of it all. And so today I still have a dream.*
> *–Martin Luther King, Jr*

Today there is hope for you. You can begin the adventure of dreaming again. Take the first steps and keep going in a sure direction. One day you will laugh and you will dance because you have a solid hope that endures.

## Discipline

Rock solid hope—the kind that will propel you forward on your journey—requires a disciplined process of discovery. This week you have the opportunity to search your heart . . . to review your past dreams and build on a new and solid foundation for the future.

Go to your favorite place to focus on finding your hope and discovering what really is inside of you. When you read something that sparks a thought, we suggest that you keep a record of it. Jot down your thoughts in the margins or in a journal so that you can review and build on them later. Although the book is organized into 31 days, you don't need to feel guilty if you don't read this book through in a month or from cover to cover. You *do* need to commit to the discipline and adventure of dreaming big.

> *Dig deeply;*
> *irrigate widely.*
> *–Kenneth L. Pike*

We challenge you to dig deeply to reach the wellspring of what really is important to you. Great treasures that you will want to pass on to your family, friends, and business associates lie below the surface of your consciousness.

Think of us as your personal trainers or life coaches that are here to help you master the process. In every chapter we will put you *in the game*. Why? You won't learn much sitting on the bench, just watching. The winning formula we want you to follow is: DISCOVER, REFINE, LIVE, TEACH, ENCOURAGE.

Will you discipline yourself to complete the exercises and Heart Probes in each chapter? When you do, you begin the adventure of discovering, refining, and living the life that really energizes you. And then you are ready to teach and encourage others to do the same.

As your trainers, we echo the coaching of Goethe, *"Begin it now."*

### *Heart Probe*

1. What were some early dreams that energized me?

2. What dreams energize me today?

3. Are my present dreams as clear as I would like them to be?
   ____YES  ____NO

4. Do I want to refine my dreams and experience the energy that derives from them?
   ____YES  ____NO

5. Are my dreams important enough for me to do the disciplined thinking necessary for clarity?
   ____YES  ____NO

# Day 3

# Shaping Your
# **Dreams**
# to Fit
# **You**

*We unintentionally undermine our efforts due
to unrealistic expectations.*
*–Margaret E. Woltjer*

## Overview

- *Environment*
- *Dollars*
- *People*
- *Geography*

## The better your dreams represent what really is in you, the more realistic they will be.

Your big dream is like your fingerprint; it is uniquely yours. You don't have to dream the dreams of your dad, mom, siblings, peers or anyone you have ever known. You will find it most satisfying when your dreams fit *you*. The process of shaping those dreams may be easier than you think . . . and even more energizing than you have imagined.

One way to get that "fit" is to put your thoughts and dreams through a filter of four dimensions—the environment you most enjoy; the amount of money implied by your dreams; the number of people you want on your team; and the psychological and geographical boundaries you envision.

## Environment

In working with a wide variety of leaders over the past three decades, I've found a very reliable principle: *people differ in the size of the setting they prefer*. Some people prefer the quiet, unrushed pace of a small town. Other people in a small town would feel like a huge gorilla in a tiny cage.

Many people work in positions far too small for both their competence and passions. In a small setting, they seem inept, like a turtle lying on its back—legs moving like crazy, but not making much progress. If they dream big dreams and pursue them, they tend to develop a maturity and passion to fit the size of their vision. I've seen it happen many times.

Bottom line: there is a setting that's right for you. If you're in too big a setting, you'll feel stressed. If you're in too small a setting, you'll feel compressed. The best dreams stretch your horizons, yet fit your worldview. What is the size of *your* ideal setting?

## Dollars

Each person has a range of dollars that they're comfortable considering in relationship to their dreams. It's a matter of identifying the amount that actually fits one's interests, vision, and sense of mission or purpose in life.

What about you? In terms of the cost of your dreams or the amount of money you want them to generate per year, check the dollar amount you are most comfortable with at this time.

- $1,000
- $10,000
- $100,000
- $1,000,000
- $100,000,000
- +

## People

By definition a dream is something that is considerably beyond your current situation. You have to stretch, grow, and sacrifice to see the dream become real. To build an organization of twelve people may seem within your scope. But to lead an organization of 12,000 may seem at this point to be a dream too large and risky.

How many people do you feel comfortable relating to, serving, selling to, or helping? How many people do you see on your team? Do you envision yourself relating to a few people and having a small, mom-and-pop kind of organization? Or do you see yourself someday leading an organization or influencing a movement of ten thousand people or maybe many more? Check the number of people you want to influence in your dreams of the future.

- ○  1–10
- ○  10–100
- ○  100–500
- ○  500–1000
- ○  1000–10,000
- ○  10,000–100,000
- ○  100,000–1,000,000
- ○  1,000,000–plus
- ○  Our society / culture
- ○  People worldwide

# Geography

What are the geographic boundaries you envision? This sounds like a big question, but it breaks down to this: do you typically think in terms of your village, town, or city? Or do you think primarily in terms of your country or in terms of the entire world? Your perspective has a great deal to do with the mental geography of your dream.

What geographic area captures your attention most of your waking hours? What piece of geography can you cope with emotionally or in what size area would you feel most comfortable? Take a minute to define the geographical boundaries of your dream world and check the size that fits you.

> **DREAMING BIG**
>
> *Vision is not dreaming the impossible dream, but dreaming the most possible dream.*
>
> —*George Barna*

- O   Neighborhood
- O   City
- O   State
- O   Multi-state region
- O   Nation
- O   World

A word of caution: Don't go to extremes. Dreams that don't fit you will not energize you. Bigger is not always better. Don't feel any pressure to set some huge, gargantuan target for the future. Paul and I are simply trying to help you define the dimensions of your dream.

Find a combination of the setting, dollars, people, and geography that truly fits you—your personality, your passions, your hopes, your desires, your dreams. Stretch a bit. Tackle something that's large enough to pull you beyond your comfort zones, but don't get into the stratosphere unless you thrive under huge pressures and challenges.

*I tell people I'm too stupid to know what's impossible.*
*I have ridiculously large dreams,*
*and half the time they come true.*
*—Debi Thomas*

To the dreamer, all dreams are big at first. As your experiences expand, so will your confidence. Seeing others like yourself achieving huge dreams will inspire you to assert, "If they can do it, so can I!"

We encourage you to think as big as you can at the present time. You can always adjust your dreams later. For now, size your dreams to the point where you have mixed emotions: *Wow!* and *I can do that!*

---

### *Heart Probe*

Recap here the *size* of your dreams.

1. What size do I really want regarding
   *Environment* _____
   *Dollars $* _____
   *People* _____
   *Geography* _____

2. How does the size of my dreams affect my emotions?
   Do I feel intimidated or energized by them?

3. What adjustments, if any, do I need to make to the size of my dreams in order to be highly motivated to pursue them?

---

# Day 4

# Sharpening the
# **Focus**
# of Your Priorities

*Some men see things as they are and say, "Why?"*
*I dream of things that never were and say, "Why not?"*
*–George Bernard Shaw*

## Overview

- *Be—Develop Personally*
- *Do—Accomplish Goals*
- *Have—Possess Things*
- *Help—Empower Others*

## Are you a "Why not?" kind of person?

Bill Bullard, an early mentor of mine, once asked, "Bobb, what would you someday like to be, do, or have?" I wrestled with that question a lot at the time, and since then I have found it to be a helpful reflection question. Over the years, I've added, "Who do you want to help?" as a fourth category. These four areas are the basis of the following *Life Focus Chart.*[1]

You will notice the phrase *"Before I die"* at the top of the chart.

I know people typically avoid thinking about their own death. But as one saint about to be martyred said, "The thought of one's own death wonderfully concentrates the mind." So let the thought of your death one day actually help you gain clarity on your *top ten* dreams related to BE, DO, HAVE, and HELP.

## Life Focus Chart
*Before I die, my top priorities are to:*

|    | BE | DO | HAVE | HELP |
|----|----|----|------|------|
| 1  |    |    |      |      |
| 2  |    |    |      |      |
| 3  |    |    |      |      |
| 4  |    |    |      |      |
| 5  |    |    |      |      |
| 6  |    |    |      |      |
| 7  |    |    |      |      |
| 8  |    |    |      |      |
| 9  |    |    |      |      |
| 10 |    |    |      |      |

You may want to copy the *Life Focus Chart* onto a flip-chart sheet of paper so you have plenty of space to make the entries you like. In each category, ask yourself, "If I had to limit my total life contribution to ten priorities in this area, what would I consider my top ten life priorities?" You do *not* have to have ten items in each column. But force yourself to prioritize to the point of having no more than ten.

After listing your BE, DO, HAVE, and HELP entries, star the top three priorities in each category. Then double star the top two and triple star the number one priority in each column. If you could only *be* one thing, what one thing would you *be*? If you could only *do* one thing, what one thing would you *do*? In the same way complete the *have* and *help* columns. You will find it helpful to *re-write your top three entries* in the following sections. In the process, you will be confirming your three strongest priorities.

## BE—Develop Personally

Many people have priorities that are primarily focused on *being*—on what kind of person they will become. Some want to be the best, the first, the fastest; others want to be free of fear or financial worry. Some want to be as fit as they used to be. Some want to be their own boss.

What are your top three personal values, character traits, or coveted roles? Review what you've written on the Life Focus Chart and jot down here in rank order the top three things you want to *be*.

Before I die, I want to *be*

1. _____
2. _____
3. _____

## DO—Accomplish Goals

Some people dream of accomplishing something, of making things happen, of *doing*. Some want to lead whole groups of people or fund a cure for cancer or help others make wise decisions.

Ask yourself, "If I had unlimited time, energy, money, education, and staff and I knew I couldn't fail . . . and I felt it was part of God's plan for me . . . what would I want to *do*?" Review the Life Focus Chart and write down your top three.

Before I die, the top three things I want to *do* are:

1. _____
2. _____
3. _____

# HAVE—Possess Things

Some people's priorities focus on what they will *have*. They want to have a certain lifestyle, live in a certain community, drive a certain car.

The downside of having things is that *they can have you* if you feel bound to them. Instead of feeling pleasure at having them, you feel panic at the thought of losing them. But in *The Good of Affluence,* John Schneider argues that the accumulation of wealth can be good for the human family if you keep things in their proper order of importance.[2] *Things* can enrich your lifestyle and be a blessing to others as well. For example, a comfortable house with enough room to entertain friends and accommodate overnight guests can bring a great deal of happiness.

> **DREAMING BIG**
>
> *We're not just building a business; we're building a legacy for our kids, and we're teaching others how to achieve their goals.*
>
> *–Neal & Mary Jo Brown*

Review the Life Focus Chart and star the top three things you want to *have*.

Before I die, I *want* to have the following:

1. _____
2. _____
3. _____

# HELP—Empower Others

A proverb says, "A good man leaves an inheritance to his children's children." In other words, part of what a good person does is to help empower others, beginning with one's own family. You make a contribution to future generations.

Beyond your family, who do you want to help? What need do you want to meet? What problem do you want to solve?

Empowering other people can take many forms:
- Rescuing those who have become victims of circumstances
- Raising children to make wise choices
- Meeting a need in society
- Teaching in the inner city
- Providing desperately needed emergency relief.

When I was with World Vision, our focus was to help people who had lost everything as a result of disasters such as flood, fire, or famine. But to do that takes huge amounts of money. Such a dream fired my creative juices and I designed the "Love Loaf" program to raise funds. The Love Loaf consisted of a little money container in the shape of a loaf of bread. You may have even had one in your church, home, or business. The Love Loaf program raised millions of dollars for world hunger relief. I found that the dream of empowering others produced enormous amounts of vital energy.

Whom do you really want to *help* in life? Which individuals, projects, or causes do you want to see gain strength because you have lived? Reviewing your chart, what are your top three?

Before I die, I want to *help* others by:

1. _____
2. _____
3. _____

The priorities you have written in this chapter likely hold clues for identifying your Life Dream in Chapter 7.

---

### *Heart Probe*

1. As I review my entries in the Life Focus Chart, what priorities actually energize me the very most?

2. What dreams received my triple star rating? Do I see a common theme?

# Day 5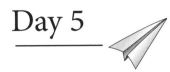

# Tapping into Your Natural **Energy**

*Ambition has at all times been the passion that best releases the energies that make civilization possible.*[1]
*–Joseph Epstein*

## Overview

- *Attitude Energy*
- *Motivation Energy*
- *Solution Energy*

## When you discover what fires your passions, you tap into a natural energy source.

*Dream energy* is a natural human energy produced whenever you have the courage to sort out what is most important to you, to explore endeavors that excite you, to follow a vision that pulls you into the future.

Consider this simple formula:

*Clear dreams = an abundance of natural energy.*
*No dreams = no natural energy.*

Dream energy is clearly distinguished from:
- nutritional energy which comes from food,
- chemical energy which comes from a B-12 shot or cup of coffee,
- social energy which comes from being with treasured friends,
- forced energy which comes from discipline.

As you reflect on your BE, DO HAVE, and HELP priorities, what would you say is your overriding ambition? What dream begins in your heart and stirs your imagination? In this chapter we explore the benefits of tapping into the natural energy that fires your passions. Chapter 6 will help you clear away any fog that remains. Chapter 7 will assist you in actually putting together your Life Dream. For now, let's focus on three reasons why discovering your Life Dream is worth every minute you give to it.

## Attitude Energy

The first benefit in pursuing a Life Dream is that it transforms your attitude about why you do what you do. An attitude is a combination of beliefs, feelings, and action tendencies. When those three components are in alignment, they produce "attitude energy." We are not talking about early in the morning until late at night "hyper energy." We mean an on-going source of stamina and optimism.

After you put together in Chapter 7 a clear Life Dream—*a vision of your future that will energize you for the rest of your life*—you will find there is a sense of refreshing, re-energizing, re-stimulating of your whole body, mind, and heart. When you are faced with obstacles, your attitude will provide an unusual ability to resolve them and get back on track . . . to move in the direction of your Life Dream.

Do we get tired sometimes? Sure. Yet we become re-energized when our thoughts, feelings, and actions connect with our dream. We think more clearly. We feel stronger, better able to tackle obstacles. We are more ready to take the next steps toward the dream.

## Motivation Energy

A second benefit in building a Life Dream is that it unlocks your internal motivation. Whereas the physical benefit of a Life Dream is physical energy, the mental benefit is on-going incentive or desire.

> **DREAMING BIG**
>
> *It isn't just about wealth and image, it's about joy—providing music and sports lessons for the children, and then having the flexibility to be there and cheer them on; traveling together and reconnecting regularly with our family in Jamaica; giving our children a foundation for pursuing their own visions; empowering others to realize their potential.*
> *–Orrett & Christine Channer*

If you don't have that motivating desire, you can create it by thinking critically and hard about what really is important to you and how you want to live your life. Write down what comes to mind, so that if your desire wanes, you can pull out what you've written and renew your motivation.

True motivation does not result from hype. "Hype"—the process of trying to convince someone they can do something they cannot do—is one of the meanest forms of manipulation. If you're five-foot tall, flat-footed, and can't jump—no matter how much you believe it, want it, and dream it—you cannot dunk a basketball . . . without the help of a mini-trampoline.

True motivation arises from within. Our focus is to help you connect with your natural, enthusiastic, internal motivation. Do you remember a day in your life when you were highly motivated? You bounded out of bed in excitement, maybe to go to Disneyland or start your summer vacation or get your diploma or get married. It was as if you had endless energy. We think this pictures *the real you*.

# Solution Energy

A third benefit in developing a Life Dream is that it enables you to solve the problems of de-motivators in life that cause you to stop pursing your dream. With the attitude and motivation you gain from your dream, you will be able to identify the de-motivators and take the necessary steps to eliminate them. Check the following that are a specific concern to you.

_____ Fear of failure
_____ Fear of success
_____ Lack of progress toward your dream or goal
_____ Trying to meet a challenge without being prepared for it
_____ Not working in your area of strength
_____ Not in control of your life
_____ Over-committed
_____ Under-resourced
_____ Too many things on your plate
_____ Feeling restricted by your job or other people
_____ Not appreciated for what you do or who you are
_____ Not enough time to do what you want to do
_____ Inadequate financial resources
_____ Lack of a clear focus on what you want to do
_____ Lack of encouragers

When one or more of these de-motivators block your path, what will you do? We can predict that most people will respond to an obstacle in one of three ways:

1. Some will take the steps necessary to overcome the block and keep going.
2. Some will change their goal to fit in with someone else's goal.
3. Some will just stop. They quit.

You have options. You can choose to use real problems to stimulate solutions. We are confident that when you have a clear Life Dream, one that you can verbalize to someone in 30 seconds or less, you will choose option one. You will approach problems with a solution orientation.

Surprisingly, a subtle form of de-motivation may come from the accomplishment of goals. Have you ever struggled night and day with high energy in attempting to complete a one to ten year project or dream? When you completed it, did you experience disorientation and a letdown in energy? Was it as if someone had pulled the plug from your energy source? Maybe you even went through some degree of depression. These are all classic indications that you were focused on and achieved a short or mid-range goal, not a Life Dream. Short-range goals give short-range energy. Mid-range goals give mid-range energy. A Life Dream gives a life-time of energy.

In the next chapter, we will focus on questions that clear away fog and prepare you to experience a lifetime of consistent energy . . . naturally.

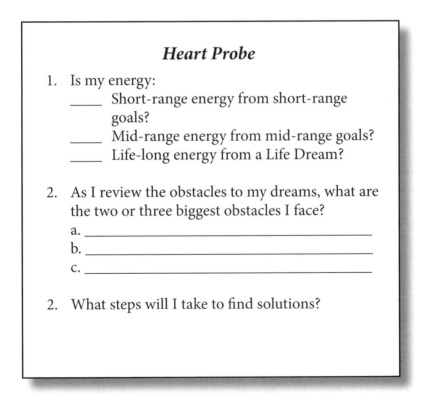

### *Heart Probe*

1. Is my energy:
   _____ Short-range energy from short-range goals?
   _____ Mid-range energy from mid-range goals?
   _____ Life-long energy from a Life Dream?

2. As I review the obstacles to my dreams, what are the two or three biggest obstacles I face?
   a. _____
   b. _____
   c. _____

2. What steps will I take to find solutions?

# Day 6

## Asking Fog-Cutting **Questions**

*A major stimulant to creative thinking is focused questions.*
*–Brian Tracy*

### Overview

- *Profound Questions*
- *Defining Moments*

### Are you absolutely confident about the focus of your life?

In this chapter we stimulate your creative thinking through focused questions. *Focusing* is essential to the process of growing into your full potential. Without focusing and getting clarity, you cannot lead. You cannot plan. And you cannot discover your Life Dream.

On the other hand, with a clear vision for your path in life, look at what you do:

- *Act with confidence*
- *Communicate effectively*
- *Motivate yourself*
- *Teach others*
- *Lead wisely.*

Here's a principle that will benefit you for life: *focus by asking.* The way to get your focus clear is by asking questions that help you think clearly. The right questions help you become a life-long student—always growing, always seeking, always clarifying the next step. Profound questions bring clarity to your dreams.

## Profound Questions

Who is the wisest person you know? Let me suggest that one of the key characteristics of this person is that he or she asks really profound, penetrating questions. I've collected questions for about thirty years, but until recently I couldn't tell you why it's so important. I didn't have the language. But here's why it's so important:

- If you ask profound questions, you get profound answers.
- If you ask shallow questions, you get shallow answers.
- If you ask no questions, you get no answers at all.

As you answer the questions that follow, we invite you to *fast write*—quickly jot down in the margins or in your journal whatever comes to mind. You will have opportunity to reflect and refine later. Don't judge your thoughts at this point. Just let the ideas flow.

## Defining Moments

To discover what is most important to you, ask yourself profound questions about your past, present, and future. There's no need to rush through this section. This could be a very revealing discovery process, even liberating and fun.

**YOUR PAST: What were the top ten most defining moments in your life?**

1. _____

2. _____

3. _____

4. _____

5. _____

6. _____

7. _____

8. _____

9. _____

10. _____

**YOUR PRESENT:** Why were you born? What would you say is your life purpose or mission in life?

_____

_____

**YOUR FUTURE:** What difference do you want to make sometime before you die?

_____

_____

Your answers to these questions are clarifying what's important to you and preparing you to finalize your Life Dream statement in the next chapter.

---

### *Heart Probe*

1. What defining moments in my past do I think will have the most impact on my future?

2. As I thought about what is important to me, what insights did I gain?

---

# Day 7

# Putting Together Your
# **Life Dream**

*We don't want enough.*
*–C.S. Lewis*

## Overview

- *Seven Characteristics of a Life Dream*
- *Starting Your Engine*
- *Life Dream Worksheet*

## What does an abundant life mean to you?

You likely are reading *Dreaming Big* because *you want more.* You have an idea of the future that motivates you, although it may be somewhat vague. You want to make a difference in life. A *Life Dream* simply helps you define what you want that difference to be.

This chapter will help you organize your thoughts from the previous chapters and guide you in putting together your own *Life Dream—a vision of your future that can energize you for the rest of your life.*

## Seven Characteristics of a Life Dream

Energy that inspires you to action will come from seven characteristics.

**1.  Your Life Dream will be born of a deep and profound desire to meet a need you see, feel, or experience.**

Typically, when you are moved by a tremendous need for something, your passion "kicks in." You see orphan children who need food and shelter; older adults who fight the ravages of a particular disease; perhaps your parents who sacrificed for you and now need financial help. You want to spend the time, energy, and money to see that need met. What are the needs that are most likely to make you weep or pound the table?

**2.  Your Life Dream will be consistent with your single greatest strength.**

What do you do best? You probably do a lot of things at an above-average level. But what is your single greatest strength—the thing you do best? Your Life Dream will build upon your greatest strength. In fact, it is probably the *central* requirement to pursue your dream.

**3.  Your Life Dream will be consistent with your values.**

The values you live by form the solid foundation upon which you can build something of consequence. According to Professor Allan Bloom, values serve not only as the basis for the routines of life, but for greatness. "Authentic values are those by which a life can be lived, which can form a people that produce great deeds and thoughts."

**4.  Your Life Dream will not make sense to or motivate some people at all.**

When I tell you my personal Life Dream is "strengthening Christian leaders world wide," you may say, "What a dull dream. That doesn't motivate me at all." My Life Dream doesn't need to motivate you—it's my dream. Your Life Dream will be uniquely yours.

As I'm writing this paragraph it's 4:30 in the morning, and I'm at Chicago O'Hare International Airport. I've been up since about midnight. I'm catching a plane at 7:00 a.m. from O'Hare to Orlando to go back home. I'm tired. I'd rather be at home sleeping. But I'm convinced that every word Paul and I write may be helpful to you and that is very exciting to me, even at this hour, because it's part of our dream to strengthen you and help you see your dreams become reality.

**5.   Your Life Dream will define the significant difference you want to make.**

A Life Dream is a call to rise above the mediocre, the average, the mundane. One of the elemental cries of the human heart is, "I don't want to just live and die. I want my life to count. I want to make a difference." Your Life Dream moves you beyond *average* living. It brings you to a higher calling, a nobler work, a significance beyond yourself. Paul and I are writing this book to help you live your dream. We believe that is a significant thing to do and therefore find it very, very energizing.

**6.   Your Life Dream will be liberating.**

Once you discover your dream, you will feel like you are on the sixteen-lane Autobahn, with no speed limit and nothing to hold you back. Your dream will not be dependent on whether or not you are downsized or fired. Your age, sex, color, and nationality will not limit you. You'll have a sense of freedom that beckons you into a future of your choosing.

**7.   Your Life Dream will be an ever-present internal reward system.**

Every step you take toward your dream will motivate—even steps that falter. You will go forward in the confidence that success is built on failure; that every failure is a stepping-stone toward your dream. Every time you do something that takes you one step closer to your dream, you experience a sense of reward within. No one has to pat you on the back. You say to yourself, "Today I know I did something significant. Today I know I made progress toward my dream."

## Starting Your Engine

If following your dreams into the future is like taking a journey, already you've explored your mental map and have an idea of your destination. Your internal compass is set by what is most important to you. Your energy fuel tank is filling up. All you need now is the right set of keys to turn on your creative engine. With these three keys, or on the *Life Dream Worksheet* that follows, your engine may roar into action and cause your heart to scream,

# *That's it! That's my Life Dream!*

## FIRST KEY: Redefine Old Dreams

We suggest you revisit areas that have been extraordinarily motivating to you in the past, determine why they were motivating, and see if you can rekindle the dream in a new way. What dreams in your past or present really energize or motivate you? Can you re-state those dreams so that they are worthy of a lifetime of energy, effort, and money?

Your ultimate dream may serve as a unifying vision for some of your smaller dreams. You may need to redefine your dream by involving more people, starting your own company, or doing what you need at work to pursue a different direction. Often defining your Life Dream is as simple as rewording something that's been a dream for years so it's clear to you that you could pursue it for a lifetime.

## SECOND KEY: If you unexpectedly inherited $10 million, what would you do?

It's a simple, but powerful question. Take it seriously. One of the reasons this question is so important is that money is the most frequent reason people limit the size of their dreams. This approach imaginatively removes the limitations of lack of money and allows

> **DREAMING BIG**
>
> *My Life Dream is to please God by learning and teaching systems of thought and action that give people freedom and hope—eternally, relationally, and financially.*
> *–Janiece S. S. Swets*

you to think/dream in a whole new way and at a whole new level.

Take 15 minutes or so and free your mind to answer the $10 million dollar question. Jot down everything that comes to your mind. Feel free to adjust the amount of money to a more realistic amount for you, but use an amount that would make you absolutely financially independent.

If I had $_____, I would _____

_____.

## THIRD KEY: Review Your Life Focus Chart

Refer to the dreams you listed on the Life Focus Chart in Chapter Four. Write here your *number one priority* in each of the BE, DO, HAVE, and HELP categories. Feel free to add new priorities or make changes. You can incorporate fresh insights you have gained this week about what really is important to you.

**I want to**

**Be** _____

**Do** _____

**Have** _____

**Help** _____

# Life Dream Worksheet

Your Life Dream statement can be as short or as long as you like. It only needs to impress you. What you write below is likely not your final draft . . . so let your self go. Jot down ideas as they come. Your statement is a work in progress. Use the following two formulas as different ways to pull your thoughts together in the formation of your one Life Dream.

## Formula One

The Life Dream (the difference I want to make before I die) that I believe is worthy of the rest of my life's time, energy, and money is:

_____

_____

_____

## Formula Two

My Life Dream is to

_____

_____

(your ultimate mission or purpose)

through my ability to

_____

_____

(your greatest strength)

that will result in

_____

_____

(the difference you want to make)

# Life Dream Check List

This dream (check all that apply)
_____ will meet the following need:

_____.

_____ is consistent with my single greatest strength, which is

_____.

_____ is consistent with what I truly believe.
_____ may not make sense to or motivate other people, but I
cannot imagine ever being bored working toward this
dream.
_____ is what I really want in life.
_____ could easily be described as "my personal life passion."
_____ is significant. It will stretch and grow me beyond my
personal comfort zones. It will cause me to rise above
mere success and contribute significance to people's lives.
_____ makes me feel energized, excited, more confident, stronger,
and eager to refine it and start developing a plan to see it
become a reality.

On your birthday, or New Year's Day, or anytime when you are
feeling out of focus, pull out a copy of this worksheet. In about ten
minutes you can regain your Life Dream perspective.

We congratulate you! You have done some hard thinking about
your past and future. Likely you have felt some strong emotions as
you delved into what is important to you. Next week, you probably
will *refine* the wording. But now you have the basics down on
paper. Cheers!

## *Heart Probe*

1. Relax. Take a minute . . . or as long as you like to kick back and enjoy the feeling of having completed a first-draft of your Life Dream. How would you describe what you feel?

2. Record it. Jot down your Life Dream, perhaps on a 3x5 card, and put it where you will be able to see it every day.

# STEP 2 → Refining Your Dream

*Begin to imagine what the desirable outcome would be like.*
*Go over these mental pictures and*
*delineate details and refinements.*
*Play them over and over to yourself.*
*—Maxwell Maltz*

Refining is the process of weeding out what is not really important and nurturing what is. It's replaying mental pictures of your future with increasing focus so that you not only *imagine* what your desirable outcome would be like . . . but you *move* toward it.

# Day 8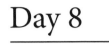

# Choosing Your
# **Direction**
# Wisely

*I shall be telling this with a sigh*
*Somewhere ages and ages hence:*
*Two paths diverged in a wood, and I—*
*I took the one less traveled by,*
*And that has made all the difference.*
*—Robert Frost*

## Overview

- *Find Your True North*
- *Exercise Your Ability to Choose*

### Do you go with the crowd or choose your own path?.

Imagine that you have come to a big choice point. As Robert Frost suggests, one path is well worn. Most people choose it. Does that make it the right path for you? Does it accurately represent the future you truly want?

Yogi Berra once said, "When you come to a fork in the road, take it." We wish it were so easy. Sometimes we panic at the thought of making a decision that will impact the course of our lives. Keep in mind that we are each "a work in process." *Refining* your Life Dream is a process that encourages mid-course corrections.

People who do not refine the direction of their lives often experience the "ladder-against-the-wrong-wall" syndrome. They climb what parents or teachers or friends tell them is a sure ladder to "success," only to find out later that the ladder is against a wall leading to a place they don't really like or believe in. Someone else's dream doesn't deliver fulfillment for you.

In this chapter, you will find help:
- Establishing a point of reference for making wise decisions,
- Gaining confidence in your unique power of choice,
- Learning how to get back on track when you lose your way.

Although these actions require real thought, they provide this confidence—*knowing that the direction you are choosing is right for you.*

## Find Your True North

A moment of choice is a moment for wisdom. It is not a time to be swayed by false promises or by what someone else wants you to do. The way to choose in freedom—not encumbered by the dictates of emotion, peer pressure, or chance—is to have a point of reference consistent with your values, attitudes, and deepest held beliefs.

> *Dad's faith is woven through his world view and all that he does. His faith is not a deep, intellectual theology, but a simple, trusting relationship with God.... It's the compass he steers by.*
> —DICK DEVOS

For thousands of years man charted his journeys with reference to the North Star because it was always the same, always dependable. He could get his bearing from the North Star and trust the direction he took. What "North Star" guides your life?

When the psalmist David thought about the consequences of

a decision he was about to make, he cried out, "Show me the path where I should walk, O Lord; point out the right road for me to follow."[1]

To find your internal North Star, ponder three essential questions until you gain confidence in your answers.

**THE QUESTION OF PURPOSE:** *Why am I here?* Does my Life Dream facilitate my sense of "mission" or "purpose" in life? Does my Life Dream represent what matters most to me?

**THE QUESTION OF PROCESS:** *If I pursue my Life Dream, then what?* Have I thought about the consequences of investing my life in my dream? Is the pursuit of my Life Dream in sync with my sense of purpose in life?

**THE QUESTION OF PASSION:** *How important is my Life Dream to me?* Do I believe in my Life Dream so deeply that I am willing to commit a lifetime of energy, time, and money to make it happen?

How did you do with these questions? For example, if your dream is to make a million by the time you are forty, is it really a Life Dream or a mid-range goal? A Life Dream needs to yield satisfying answers to all three questions.

If as a result of these questions you're not satisfied with the way you stated your Life Dream, *that's a good sign.* It simply means the clarifying process has already begun. By the end of this week, you will be much further along. Be patient with yourself because when you finally get your Life Dream right, you will know it. You will feel the energy. You will have confidence that the direction of your life is significant.

---

**DREAMING BIG**

*The American Dream is that every man must be free to become whatever God intends he should become.*

—Ronald Reagon

---

## Exercise Your Ability to Choose

Most of us tend to get off track and foggy about our purpose in life. We fall into ruts of thinking and behavior. We get focused on urgent but low-importance activities that drain all of the available energy. Items on our To-Do list overwhelm us. We get beaten down, worn down, run down, fatigued, exhausted. We tend to settle for less than our full potential. The result? We respond in predictable but unfortunate ways to the stimuli we face. For example, we quit or give in to the demands of a boss for overtime. Or we carry work frustrations home, and the slightest provocation can set off angry explosions against those we love most.

We can diagram this type of behavior this way:

---

### Stimulus ➤ Response

---

Like psychologist Pavlov's famous experiment with dogs, we can show a certain validity to the S > R theory. Do we have to think about removing our hand from a hot burner? No, we instantly respond. The stimulus produces a predictable response. But what about bigger issues in our lives, like following our dream and living our values? Are we bound to live an S > R type of existence as some suppose?

Paul and I don't think so. The good news is you have the freedom to choose the direction you want to go. One of the most intriguing lectures my friend Paul experienced was when his psychology professor said the S > R theory was far too limited. Although it does explain some human behavior, it says nothing about human choice. A more accurate description can be diagramed this way:

---

### Stimulus ➤ FREEDOM TO CHOOSE ➤ Response

---

Stephen Covey writes that this concept of choice also had a profound impact on his life and was a fundamental concept to his work on the 7 Habits. While in a library, he took a book from the shelves and read three sentences that "staggered him to the core:"

*Between stimulus and response there is a space.*
*In that space lies our freedom and power to choose our response.*
*In those choices lie our growth and our happiness.*[2]

If you notice that certain stimuli (people, situations, job environment) have influenced you to respond in a way that is unwise and contrary to your Life Dream, you can change the pattern. In the space between stimulus and response, you can insert your ability to think, your freedom to choose. You can choose what you really want to think about. You can choose what you truly want to do. You can pursue what is most important to you.

---

**Negative Influence ➤ WISE CHOICE ➤ Forward Progress**

---

When negative influences are intercepted by wise choices, you are in a better position to make forward progress toward your dreams. And as you exercise your freedom to choose, you may even rethink your lifework. Wow! That could be huge. It's the focus of our next chapter.

## *Heart Probe*

1. On a scale of 1 to 10, how confident am I in the direction I want to go? _____

2. What did I learn about me from asking the questions of Purpose, Process, and Passion?

3. What choices would it be wise for me to make today?

# Day 9

# Rethinking Your **Lifework** Based on Your **Life Dream**

> *Good is the enemy of great.*
> *—Jim Collins*

## Overview

- *Bogged Down*
- *Climbing Out*
- *Breaking Through*

## How good do you have it?.

If you are like most Americans, you have a job . . . and if you're married . . . so does your spouse. You can put food on the table. You have a few friends, two cars that start, and maybe a big screen TV. Pretty good. The American Dream. Right?

Let's think about it. Many people do not strive to have a great life because they have a *good* life. They do not work at having a great marriage because they have a *good* marriage. They may not have great family time because they have some *good* times. They may not have great work to do, because they have *good* work to do.

## Bogged Down

Although our lives look good on the outside, we may not feel good on the inside. Unless we have cheerleaders who urge us on, we gradually settle in for "the way things are." We begin to say, "Well, maybe the dream wasn't realistic. Maybe I don't have that kind of potential. Maybe it's just easier to stay in my current job. Maybe it's easier to do the same thing all my friends are doing."

All of a sudden we find ourselves settling for just a part of what we could become or achieve. Without a Life Dream we tend to get bogged down.

## Climbing Out

In his book, *Good to Great*, Jim Collins writes, "It is impossible to have a great life unless it is a meaningful life. And it's very difficult to have a meaningful life without meaningful work."[1]

Are you wondering if your current job is meaningful work? A number of clients I've talked to over the last few years remarked that even though they are successful in their careers, these careers are not necessarily what they want to do for the rest of their lives. They are seeking what I refer to as their "Lifework." Around mid-life, the search for meaningful work may approach the nature of quiet desperation . . . or resignation.

Men and women in the midst of a mid-life crisis say things like this:

"I guess I'm just a jack of all trades and a master of none."

"I'm still trying to figure out what I want to be when I grow up."

"I'm not doing what I plan to do someday, but I haven't figured out what that is yet."

If you are uncertain about the direction of your life, the Lifework concept may help clarify the issues. It simply illustrates the life progressions many commonly go through: Job, Career, and Lifework. *Moving into your Lifework will be the most direct path to your Dream.*

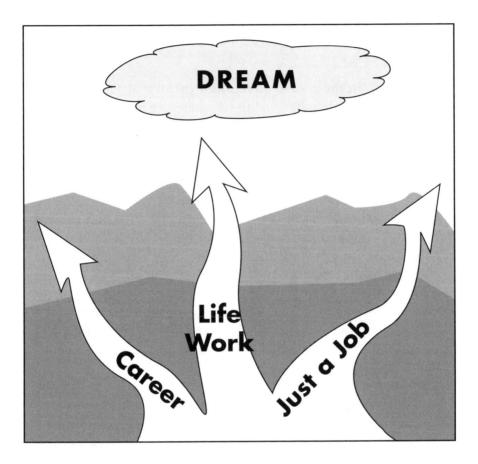

On the way to clarifying our *Lifework,* some get stuck in a *success syndrome*—feeling that success means out-of-control accumulation. They conclude that they may as well get all the *things* they can out of life because life gives them very little in return. They make drastic lifestyle changes such as overspending, bizarre clothing, and body makeovers. The result? A sometimes tragic midlife crisis—a frenzy of the mind or of activity that has no meaning or direction.

## Breaking Through

If you want to find the best use of the rest of your life, if you want to break through barriers that keep you from a meaningful life, measure your current work with the following components of a Lifework.

1. **You work in the area of your single greatest strength.**

   You will remember that in Chapter 7 we mentioned that working in the area of your greatest strength is one of the characteristics of a Life Dream. Do you have a clear view of your single greatest strength? Most of us know a lot of things we do fairly well, but typically do not see what we do best.

   I once attended a conference where Dr. Peter Drucker repeated that question, "What do you do best"? I came up with my top three and still couldn't figure out which of the three was my single greatest strength. So I went to a trusted friend, and he helped me figure it out. If you find it difficult to identify your single greatest strength, make a list of five to ten things you feel are possibilities. Rank them. Take the top three and have a friend help you identify number one. Whatever your Lifework turns out to be, it will maximize your single greatest strength.

2. **You never tire of it.**

   You may get tired while doing your Lifework, but you love what you see as a result. I get tired and fatigued consulting, but I never tire of seeing clarity and confidence instead of fogginess in people's eyes. During your late thirties and early forties, as you look ahead to twenty or thirty more years of active work, you must believe that this work is a worthy use, a noble use, the best use of your life.

3. **You feel affirmed.**

   Maybe many things you did in the past just didn't seem to fit. Your honest friends might have said, "I don't think you will be doing this long. I don't think it is really you." When you find your Lifework, your closest friends will say, "Aha! You have found your true niche." You will have a sense of well-being.

4. **You are rewarded financially.**

You must be able to make a living with your Lifework. If you can't, you can consider it a life hobby or a retirement pastime, but it cannot be considered your Lifework.

If you have identified an area you hope will become your Lifework but right now you can't make a living at it, don't be discouraged. Keep at it. Keep asking yourself the question, "What could I do today to start earning a living doing what I enjoy the most?"

5. **You feel fulfilled.**

The word *fulfillment* is probably the single greatest buzzword for people who are trying to sort out their Lifework. Lack of fulfillment is the reason $500,000-per-year salaried executives resign from corporate America to teach college for $60,000 per year or take lower salaries at other companies offering new challenges.

Coming to clarity on this subject is typically not an easy task, but well worth the effort! You'll detect an internal harmony knowing that your work is consistent with the way God designed you. And when you define your Lifework, you have taken a huge step forward in clarifying your Life Dream!

> **DREAMING BIG**
>
> *I literally see my work as prayer. I am so involved in what I do that everything feels like an act of service.*
>
> —BERNICE LEDBETTER

## *Heart Probe*

1. As I review the charastics of Lifework, do they describe my current work?

2. Do I feel that my current work is leading me toward my Life Dream or away from it?

3. If I feel I need to refine my Lifework, what actions would it be wise for me to take now?

# Day 10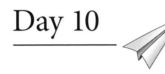

# Funding Your
# **Dreams**

*A person can be highly educated,*
*professionally successful,*
*and financially illiterate.*
                    *–Robert T. Kiyosaki*

## Overview

- *Invest in Yourself*
- *Consider Your Options*

## How do you plan to fund your dreams?

A lot of people have dreams, but they don't have a way to reach them. I may want desperately to win the roses at the Kentucky Derby, but without a thoroughbred I can't do it! Even Willie Shoemaker, the jockey who reportedly made $54 million in his career, wouldn't have made a nickel riding on a broken-down plow horse. Some people are world-class jockeys riding organizational horses that aren't ever going to get them to the finish line on time.

Do you have investments that can adequately resource your dreams? If not, what financial options do you have for pursing your dreams?

## Invest in Yourself

Before we get into the specifics of what you need to fund a dream, let me share with you an introductory perspective on funding.

I'll never forget meeting Mr. Meirs. He had served on the board of directors of seven Fortune 500 companies and, in his retirement years, was the financial advisor for a consortium of doctors. He had just closed on multimillion-dollar acreage on the Atlantic for a new hotel that the doctors were building.

As I began to sense the scope of his business acumen, I asked, "If you were me, where would you suggest I invest?" His counsel shaped my investment strategy from that time to this. He said, "If I were you, *I would invest in myself.* I would have a nice home, get it paid off as quickly as possible, and invest in my own dreams and ideas." He continued, "Trust your own dreams; invest in your own dreams. That's where you'll have the ability to keep track of your money and make decisions that affect your family's future."

Does Mr. Meirs' counsel apply to you? Consider investing a percentage of your hard-earned money in your own dreams. To paraphrase a popular phrase, "Put your money where your dream is!"

## Consider Your Options

In his best-selling book, *Rich Dad, Poor Dad*, Robert Kiyosaki suggests that income normally is generated in four ways.

1. You can be an employee.
2. You can be self-employed.
3. You can invest capital.
4. You can own a business system.[1]

Kiyosaki's "poor dad" told him to pursue the first two options. Perhaps your dad told you the same thing: "Get a good education so you can get a decent paying job." The basic idea was to *work for money*, to trade hours for dollars. But there is a downside. As an employee, you lose personal freedom. Somebody tells you when to come to work, when to have lunch, when you can go home, how much you can make, when . . . or if . . . you will get a raise. You are at the mercy of somebody else's goals, dreams, and values.

Doctors, lawyers, and other self-employed professionals face constraints as well. What they have in common with the employee is *trading hours for dollars*. If they stop working, the money stops flowing. They might not get fired, but often work long hours. Traditional business owners usually participate in the hours for dollars routine. Often their business owns them.

In contrast to Kiyosaki's "poor dad," his "rich dad" taught him how to pursue investing and owning a business. The basic idea is to have *money work for you*. The concept sounds great, but both investing capital and starting your own business from scratch normally require large amounts of capital not available to most people. So what can the average person do to fund their dream?

In an interview entitled, *The Perfect Business*, Kiyosaki points to network marketing or private franchising as a brilliant way for the average person to keep his daytime job while building a business income. A private franchise has features similar to those of a public franchise—a carefully developed business model and training system. The big advantage of a private franchise is that you get a proven business system plus training without a huge capital investment. "You'll spend some years in sweat equity," declared Kiyosaki, "but you will be building a very big asset that can set you financially free."[2]

Developing an income stream beyond your job requires learning delayed gratification. It requires stamina, focus, and mental toughness. You can't be bullied by the discouraging words of well-meaning souls who may think they have your best interest at heart. They likely do not know your interior core—the dreams and passions and courage that drive and pull you into the future.

To fund your dream, think of ways to expand your income rather than shrink your dreams. *Multiple income streams make sense in today's financial environment* because if one stream dries up due to job loss or disability, you will have at least one other to depend on. Investigate what is available to you. Identify what you need to know and explore it diligently. [3]

## *Heart Probe*

1. Realistically, am I financially literate in regard to my dreams?
   o Yes
   o No
2. What financial advisor could coach me to the next level?

3. What books do I need to read to achieve financial peace?

# Day 11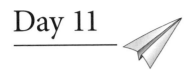

# Developing a
# **Strategic Plan**

*Strategy means making clear-cut choices
about how to compete.[1]*

*–Jack Welch*

## Overview

- *Short and Long-Range Plans*
- *Dream Priorities and Your Job*
- *Developing a Clear Strategy*
- *Strategy Worksheet*
- *Smart Planning Leads to Action*

### Is the chicken or the egg most important?

On the way to the Super Bowl, do you need a strong offense or a strong defense? To energize your life, do you need a clear dream or a clear plan? Obviously, both are required. A plan can be well organized, but without a dream, it's like an electrical cord that isn't connected to the energy source. Although a clear dream energizes you, a strategic plan helps you make clear-cut choices about how to compete against obstacles . . . and win.

## Short and Long-Range Plans

Plans are like a stairway to your dreams—a step-by-step guide that begins now and outlines what to do next. Clear plans produce action that is realistic, measurable, and time-dated.

Bill Anderson, shared an important insight on long-term thinking. "You know, Bobb, I find that the leader typically has a good grasp of reality and a clear dream of what will be someday, but most people need practical, close-in, ninety-day to one-year measurable plans." We agreed it's best to set clear short-range plans in the context of long-range plans.

## Dream Priorities and Your Job

In both your short and long range plans, you will need to address the relationship between your job and your dream. Perhaps you feel discouraged about your job thinking, "My job has no connection to my dream." Maybe. But is it possible to rethink your perspective so that your present situation becomes a *learning opportunity for the future?*

Ask yourself the following questions:

- What lessons could I learn in my present position that might propel me in the pursuit of my dream?
- Who do I know that might help me make progress toward my dream?
- Is my current financial position adequate for funding my dream right now? If so, for how long? If not, what other options do I have?

In the context of your current work situation, select the dream for which you want to develop a strategic plan and complete the following worksheet.

> **DREAMING BIG**
>
> *I believe that children get a very different upbringing when their parents stay close. So my dream now is to have a lot of mothers come home and raise their children, to have more peace of mind.*
>
> —LATA GALA

# Personal Strategy Worksheet

Dream _____

Today's Date_____

**Purpose:** Why is this dream important to me?


**Roadblocks:** What three things could keep me from pursuing my dream?

    1.

    2.

    3.


**Resources:** What three key resources will help me get past the roadblocks?

    1.

    2.

    3.


**Priorities:** What measurable results do I want to achieve and by what date?

    1.

    2.

    3.


**Actions:** What are my next steps to achieve these results?

    1.

    2.

    3.

## Smart Planning Leads to Action

Some of us have spent a great amount of time making plans—but then we file them away and forget them. Thinking *plus acting* gets results. Henri Bergson put it this way, "Think like a man of action, act like a man of thought." Use your freedom of choice to act, not merely react. We focus on how to do that in the next chapter.

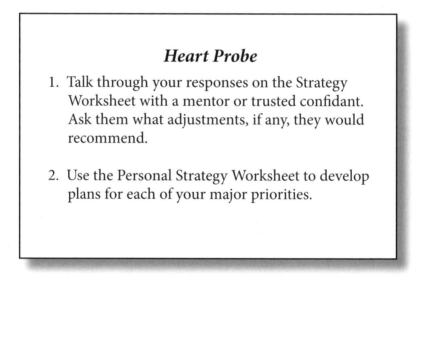

### *Heart Probe*

1. Talk through your responses on the Strategy Worksheet with a mentor or trusted confidant. Ask them what adjustments, if any, they would recommend.

2. Use the Personal Strategy Worksheet to develop plans for each of your major priorities.

# Day 12

## Turning
# Dream Energy
## into
# Results

*There are basically two types of people.
People who accomplish things, and
people who claim to have accomplished things.
The first group is less crowded.*

*–Mark Twain*

### Overview

- *Building Your Confidence*
- *Maintaining Your Focus*
- *Visualizing Your Success*
- *Taking Your Next Step*

### Do you accomplish what you want to do?

Perhaps you would like to be the type of person who accomplishes goals, but things happen. You may have failed to achieve something important to you and now you cannot see yourself succeeding. You may keep busy, but you don't get much done. You don't know how to take the next step toward your dreams.

If you believe you are not made for sitting still, if you feel an inner drive to get up and do something significant, if you are committed to defeating habits of inertia, you are ready for turning your dream energy into confidence-building action.

## Building Your Confidence

Taking even small, imperfect steps in the direction of your dreams begins a confidence-building process. The experience of my writing partner is a case in point.

One of Paul's dreams in college was to become a successful speaker. But as you may know, the number one fear for most Americans is speaking in front of a group of people. Although terrified by the prospect of public speaking, Paul's dream persisted. He began a course of action to counteract his fear.

First, he *realized he needed practice*. He wrote down some thoughts and went to a noisy boiler room in the lower level of a building and shut the door so no one could hear him. He imagined the various pipes in the room as individuals waiting with rapt attention to what he would say. The engine noise in the room meant he had to project his voice. He began with faltering stops and miscues and wrong words and mispronunciations. But the pipes and engines didn't care. They just "clamored" for more. Day after day he kept at it until the words began to flow and the verbal humps smooth.

> *I have seen countless people make a choice to be confident. If you don't naturally feel bold and confident, you can choose an attitude of confidence.*
> —RICH DEVOS

Second, he *looked for a coach*. On a bulletin board in the Hope College Speech Department, he found notice of a speech contest and an experienced professor who would help prepare contestants. He decided to enter the contest and learn what he could. The professor was a wise coach who encouraged Paul by telling him what he was doing right. He showed him what to do next. He challenged him to keep going. To everyone's amazement, Paul eventually won the state oratorical contest in Michigan and placed fifth in the nation. Practice and coaching enabled him to overcome his fears.

*Action conquers fear.* When you chose to act confidently, you are more likely to overcome fear and turn dream energy into results. *Results*, in turn, increase your confidence. So we coach you to determine what your next step is and then take it. You will find that making progress toward your dream, even when the steps seem small, builds your confidence.

## Maintaining Your Focus

Persistent action toward your dreams keeps you focused. You learn to fight distractions. You find creative ways to keep your focus sharp—pictures on your refrigerator, songs that fire you up, recordings that inspire, a voice mail message to yourself, copies of your Life Dream in every room of the house—daily reminders of your Life Dream.

Paul keeps a copy of his Life Dream on the visor of his car. Part of it reads: "to be part of what God is doing in changing the world, one person at a time." Being reminded of his Life Dream energizes him during the tedium of driving to appointments. It expands his vision of his "world." It reminds him of the significance of every person he meets. It challenges him to keep going in the direction of his dream.

In addition to a visual reminder of your Life Dream, keep a copy of your *Strategy Worksheet* from Day 11 where you can view it daily. As you think about your strategy, ask yourself:

1.  Do I really have a clear vision about what matters most to me?

2.  Do I understand the obstacles I face and how to get through them? If not, what books do I need to read? Who could coach me? What can I do today, this week, that will propel me toward my dream?

3. Am I passionate enough about my Life Dream to work toward it now? If not, what is blocking me?

4. How might fear be holding me back? What actions do I need to take to overcome my fear?

5. Is my next step clear? If not, how can I revise it so it's crystal clear?

6. Am I making progress?

As you assess your situation, you may find that you allow *other people* to destroy your focus. Your *boss* is too demanding of your time. Your *spouse* does not buy into your dream. Your *friends* make fun of your efforts to fulfill your dream. *The temptation is always there to blame someone else for one's own inactivity or failure.* Although people and situations certainly do present major challenges, find one or two things you *can* do. When you act on what is possible, you defy those forces that would bring you down. You refuse to let people bully you. You take charge of your own life instead of giving in to the demands or ridicule of others.

If you're married, you will need to win your spouse's support. What good is accomplishing your dream at the expense of your marriage and family? If you learn to reach the heart of your spouse, you will have the foundation skill to reach the heart of others.

## Visualizing Your Success

One powerful motivator to action is to envision your dream being fulfilled. What does it look like to you? Do you let yourself daydream about your Life Dream? For Walt Disney, it was not mere hype to declare, "If you can dream it, you can do it." He "saw" Disney World before he built it.

What picture or object or blueprint represents your dream to you? See it. Touch it. Feel it. Smell, taste, and listen to it if you can. Let your dream-focused imagination sweep you forward into action.

## Taking the Next Step

On the way from a client's office to a car rental agency in Chicago, the limo driver talked to me about his admiration for men who started on the streets and became world famous boxers. He admired anyone who was willing to pay the price. He said, "Most people want things, but they're unwilling to do the work to get them. Basically, they're only wishful thinkers wanting people to hand things to them."

> *Skill to do comes from doing.*
> —RALPH WALDO EMERSON

All dreams require discipline—*the regulation of behavior to act on what we have learned.* As Pat Williams puts it, discipline is "simply doing something you don't want to do in order to achieve something you want to achieve."[1] In the personal discovery exercises of Week 1, you *discovered* what is most important to you and how to choose appropriate actions. This week, you're disciplining yourself with new insights, new confidence, and new sense of urgency to take the next step and further *refine* your dreams and actions.

As you take the next step, remember that a great looking Dream Strategy not acted upon stands *no* chance for fulfillment; but an imperfect Dream Strategy that is acted upon has *every* chance of success. We echo what Coach John Wooden would tell his players, "Don't let what you cannot do interfere with what you can do."

## *Heart Probe*

1. What will I do this week, tomorrow, or right now to build confidence in myself and my dream?

2. Am I satisfied with my answers in the section on Maintaining Your Focus?  If not, what actions will I take?

3. What will I do to visualize my success?

4. What is my next step toward my dream?

# Day 13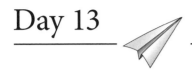

# **Balancing**
## Your Life

*What good will it be for a man if he gains the whole world,*
*yet forfeits his soul?* [1]

*–Jesus*

### Overview
- *Warning Signs*
- *Balancing Life's Dimensions*
- *The Integrated Life*

## Is your life balanced and integrated right now?

In *Death of a Salesman,* playwright Arthur Miller depicted
Willy Loman as a man selling his soul to "materialism"—the belief
that your worth and the value of life are defined by money and
material things. Loman tried to pass on these values to his sons and
in the process destroyed himself, and their lives as well. After their
father's suicide, the sons concluded, "He had the wrong dreams."

Wrong dreams reflect a tragic imbalance in our lives. *Life
balance,* on the other hand, is the process of *correcting imbalance*
and *integrating our dreams* according to a healthy framework
of values. When we don't get the balance right, we feel out of

sync with others and even ourselves. Life's demands overwhelm, relationships start to break, and physical symptoms become painful. We sense we are missing joy and purpose in life . . . and we don't know where to find them. We feel we have lost integrity at the interior core of our being.

Shelley Baur, entrepreneur and champion for the cause of personal integrity, reflects on a time when her life was out of balance.

> *I recognized that I had sold myself and everyone else on a package that looked great. But I had headaches and other physical symptoms of living a life that was out of integrity.* [2]

Imagine one of sculptor Alexander Calder's beautiful mobiles—the art that hangs on strings or wires—with various pieces balancing and floating on the wind. If you were to add a weight to one of the pieces, the rest of the pieces would contort into ugliness. Life can be that way. When we put all the weight of our energy, planning, time, and money into one area, we find ourselves with no time for other key areas. Life lacks beauty and harmony and balance.

The changes can be subtle. Those in the midst of personal imbalance may not see the connections between damaged relationship and working eighty hours a week, or financial loss and laziness, or heart problems and their poor eating and exercise habits. They don't see the warning signs.

## Warning Signs

Like a tire out of round, signs that our lives are out of balance start out with a barely noticeable thump, thump, thump. Gradually the thump becomes louder and impossible to ignore. We could choose to drown out the warning signals of danger ahead with distractions, busyness, alcohol, or "blind ambition." Or we could welcome the warnings as a spur to take corrective action.

How balanced is your life? To find out, run the following diagnostics test on your life and honestly answer YES or NO to these questions.[3]

_____ Is each family member happy with the amount of attention I give them?

_____ Am I confident I will have adequate income when I retire?

_____ Do I find fulfillment in the work I do?

_____ Do I feel "emotionally connected" to my friends and business associates?

_____ Do I know for sure that I have a "right relationship" with God?

_____ Can I point to any personal growth in the past year; any evidence of becoming more knowledgeable, more patient, more skillful, more willing to take risk?

_____ Is my sleep restful and free of anxious thoughts?

_____ Do I feel energetic, healthy, and physically fit?

If you answered NO to *any* of the questions above, you may be hearing the thumping warnings of imbalance. If so, ask yourself, "How can I regain balance?"

## Balancing Life's Dimensions

For a number of years it seemed to me that life was like a puzzle with ten thousand places to put all the pieces. The task of balancing them felt overwhelming. Then I began to realize there are actually only eight categories into which all those pieces fit. Eight pieces can be managed.

These are the eight categories or dimensions of life that need to remain in fundamental balance:

- Family—your immediate and extended family
- Financial—your money, investments, and debt concerns
- Vocational—your career or work activity
- Social—your friends, social clubs, civic activities
- Spiritual—your relationship with God

- Mental—your reading, learning, and personal growth goals
- Emotional—your feelings of love, anger, hope, anxiety, confidence, etc.
- Physical—your exercise, nutrition, recreation.

I have found it helpful to actually chart my priorities in each of these eight categories. The following *Balance Chart* provides a framework for organizing/balancing plans. Every plan you have likely fits somewhere on the chart. If need be, copy the chart onto a piece of paper large enough to hold all of the elements.

For this exercise, let's begin with your dreams from Chapter 4— your BE, DO, HAVE, HELP dream list. As you chart these dreams, you will be using three time frameworks:

① Short-Range—priorities you estimate will take less than a year to achieve;

② Mid-range—priorities you estimate will take a year to ten years to achieve;

③ Long-range—priorities you want to accomplish sometime before you die.

Take an hour or so at a park, by a river, by a lake, in the woods, in the mountains, at your favorite restaurant, or wherever you go to relax and fill out this chart completely. Look at each of your dreams and ask, "In which of the eight areas of life does this dream fit, and when do I realistically see this dream being accomplished? What is the time frame?" Add other dreams that come to mind.

Once you've got the chart filled out, you'll be able to visualize whether your life is in balance. If you find that you have a large number of work related priorities, but no family and marriage priorities at all, or lots of financial priorities and no personal growth priorities, ask yourself, "What are my priorities in those empty areas on the chart?" Used this way, the chart helps identify imbalance *and* create balance.

Now that you have more of your priorities/dreams listed, are you able to take one more step toward clarity? On a scale of 1 to 10 (1 is hardly committed at all and 10 is deeply committed), pencil in the numbers that reflect your commitment level to each of the priorities/dreams in the chart.

# Life Balance Chart

| Categories Of Life | Short-Range Priorities<br>Measurable<br>*(one year or less)* | Mid-Range Priorities<br>Measurable<br>*(one to ten years)* | Long-Range Priorities<br>Non-Measurable<br>*(before I die)* |
|---|---|---|---|
| **Family** | | | |
| **Financial** | | | |
| **Vocational** | | | |
| **Social** | | | |
| **Spiritual** | | | |
| **Mental** | | | |
| **Emotional** | | | |
| **Physical** | | | |

## The Integrated Life

Another way to balance our lives is to look at the *organizing principle* at the center of our lives. What is at the center is what is most important to us and will affect every dimension of life. Sometimes that center is one's own ego or self.

Willy Loman is an example of an ego-driven life. Loman had all money could buy, but felt lonely, empty, unfulfilled, and terribly sad. His ego was his god—it organized, but ruined his life. It killed him.

Billionaire Rich DeVos reflected on the limitations of wealth: "A poor man might live with the delusion that if he only had enough money all his problems would disappear. When he acquires a fortune, he discovers just how limited money can be. Money cannot buy peace of mind. It cannot heal ruptured relationships or build meaning into a life that has none. It cannot relieve guilt or speak to the great agonies of the broken heart."[4]

Have you thought about what is at the center of your life? Paul and I find the following chart helpful in reflecting how whatever we place at the center of our lives affects all eight dimensions of life. We can view this model as follows:

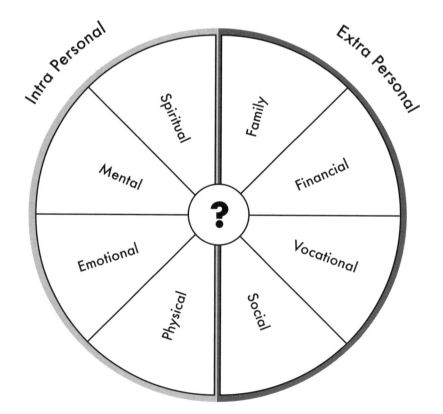

According to German theologian, Dietrich Bonhoeffer, the only rightful place for God in a human's life is at the center. It is "not God at the end of one's rope or in failure or in death or as a last resort, but God at the centre."[5] Rich DeVos concludes, "When you reach the end of your earthly life, what good will money and fame do you? In this life, there is only one thing we can ultimately depend on, and that is God Himself."[6]

If you had the opportunity to speak to graduating seniors—or to share deeply with your own children at a milestone in their lives—what would you say? Speaking on *"The Power of a Dream"* at a baccalaureate service, Dr. Sanders L. Willson revealed to the seniors one of the passions of his heart. "I plead with you to fulfill the purpose for which you were made . . . to be a people who dream, but dream in a way that pleases God—not only in the context of your abilities, but in the context of His ability to fulfill your dream—by *not* underestimating your potential, by *not* overestimating your development, and by *not* leaving God out of your lives."[8]

> *If the ego governs absolutely, then a person loses his vital balance and is ruled solely by his own tastes and needs— and becomes hostile to his own nature."[7]*
> —NORMAN COUSINS

As you reflect on your life, what do you want the "center" of your life to be? Does your Life Dream exhibit the kind of integrating center you want? Will it nourish your soul?

### *Heart Probe*

1.  What do I want to be the unifying core or center in my life?

2.  Is there a way to rewrite my Life Dream so that it incorporates this unifying center of my life?

3.  What can I begin to implement today to achieve more balance in my life?

# Day 14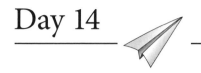

# **Stretching** beyond Childhood **Labels**

*We cannot become what we need to be...*
*by remaining what we are.*
*–Max DePree*

## Overview
- *Identifying Past Labels*
- *Assessing Our True Value*
- *Becoming What We Need to Be*

## What do you need to be?

Perhaps you still remember the pain you felt when a parent or teacher or some peer said,
—You'll never amount to anything!
—You're stupid!
—You're ugly!
—I don't want *you* on my team!
Your own perception about your potential may have been harsh.

You tried something and failed. You told yourself, "I can't ever do anything right. I might as well not even try."

> We grow through our dreams. All great men and women are dreamers.
> —WOODROW WILSON

But now you have a dream of doing something that pulls you into new growth opportunities beyond what you once thought possible. Your dreams inspire you to imagine yourself beyond your emotional comfort zone, beyond your phobias, beyond any limiting childhood labels. They motivate you to forge a new future, a new identity.

## Identifying Past Labels

We urge you to take a candid look at your childhood labels. One way to do that is to organize descriptions of yourself under the categories of "Just a Dreamer" or "Anything but a Dreamer." In the following chart, check the boxes under either description that applied to you as a child. Then put an X in front of the description that applies to you now. If you think both descriptions on a line apply to you, determine which one is dominant. You may even find that as an adult you are the opposite of the way adults saw you in childhood. Either way is okay!

| A Dreamer | Not a Natural Dreamer |
|---|---|
| o Originator–visionary | o Maximizer of what exists now |
| o Imagines the future with ease | o Has some difficulty imagining the future |
| o Dreams 5–50 years into the future | o Plans 1-2 weeks into the future |
| o Spice of life | o Salt of the earth |
| o Risk taker | o Prudent |

| A Dreamer | Not a Natural Dreamer |
|---|---|
| o Flexible | o Stable |
| o Original creativity; starts with blank sheet of paper | o Adaptive creativity; starts with proven models |
| o Theme: If it has been done before, why do it that way again? | o Theme: Why reinvent the wheel? |
| o Someday | o Yesterday, today |
| o Abstract, intuition | o Concrete, facts |
| o Head in the clouds | o Feet on the ground |
| o Pioneer of the new | o Protector of the proven |
| o Excited about change | o Resistant to unnecessary change |
| o Avant-garde | o Traditional |
| _____ boxes checked | _____ boxes checked |

If you see yourself now mostly in the "Dreamer" category, you likely have all kinds of ideas about what you would like to do in the future. You get excited about possibilities. Tell yourself to slow down and reflect on the wisest course of action for you. You may need to go back to chapter eleven and discipline yourself to actually write a clear strategy for your future.

If you see yourself now as "Not a Natural Dreamer," you probably already have all of your ideas in a framework of your own choosing. You are likely very organized and buttoned down in this area. Remind yourself to be open to new possibilities about who you are and what you can become.

## Assessing Our True Value

People assess their value in different ways. We offer you here three views. First, Buckminster Fuller, a philosopher, architect, and city planner, focused on the complex engineering of the human body in this paraphrase of his self-description.

*I am a self-balancing, twenty-eight-jointed biped, an electrochemical processing plant with integrated and separate facilities for maintaining energy in storage batteries for the subsequent powering of thousands of hydraulic and pneumatic pumps, each with their own motors attached; sixty-two thousand miles of small blood vessels, millions of warning-signal devices, railroads, and conveyor systems; plus crushers and cranes, a widely distributed telephone system needing no service for seventy years if well maintained; all guided from a turret in which are located telescopes, microscopic, self-registering range finders, a spectroscope, et cetera.*[1]

Second, C. S. Lewis, a professor of literature and best-selling author, argues that there are "no ordinary people" because one of the qualities that gives human beings value is that we were created to be immortal. "You have never talked to a mere mortal. Nations, cultures, arts, civilizations—these are mortal, and their life is to ours as the life of a gnat."[2]

Third, the psalmist David, an ancient king, poet, and musician, reviewed the intricacies of the human body and concluded, "*I am fearfully and wonderfully made.*"[3]

What is your assessment of yourself? Do you realize that you have an essential value way beyond the number of zeros in your salary or any achievements you have accomplished? You are "wonderfully made." What you accomplished in the past or will in the future is nothing compared to who you already are.

## Becoming What We Need to Be

Your true value as a human being provides a solid foundation for developing your potential. Think about this for a moment. If you had a $1,000,000.00 plus annual residual income, what would you do differently? Consider your background, your opportunities, your confidence level, your fears, your desire to grow, your work situation, your big dreams . . . consider everything. What do you feel, think, and see as your ultimate potential? What could you possibly do or become? What position could you hold? What level of leadership could you take? What could you accomplish?

> *In each of us are places where we have never gone. Only by pressing the limits do we ever find them.*
> —JOYCE BROTHERS

Take an hour away if you need to. Go down by the river or to your favorite coffee shop—any place where you can think and not be distracted. Take your laptop, PDA, or paper and pen with you to answer the questions in the paragraph above. In the process you'll answer this crucial question: *Dreaming big, what could I become? How does that affect the statement of my Life Dream?*

Welcome back. You might feel overwhelmed by your ideas. That's how I felt at one period of my life. I have always been a dreamer and sometimes felt overwhelmed by the number of things I wanted to do. When I was in my twenties, one of my mentors, Sam Miller, taught me a life-changing principle. After listening to my dreams, he said, "Bobb, it's the rare person who will take a few good ideas and develop them to their logical conclusion." That was his main challenge to me: *Take a few good ideas and develop them to their full potential.*

> *The measure of greatness is not where we have been but where we want to go.*
> —NORMAN COUSINS

We offer you the counsel Sam gave me. Make a complete list of your ideas. Then choose one or two or three great ideas you want to develop with the help of the Strategy Work Sheet in Chapter 11. Use a clean sheet of paper for each idea. This is the best strategy we know to move in a surefooted way toward your dreams.

## *Heart Probe*

1.  On a scale of 1 to 10 (10 being absolute clarity), how clear am I on the following?

    _____ I know who I am.

    _____ I know what my potential is.

    _____ I know where I want to go.

2.  Incorporating what I learned this past week, how should I now restate my Life Dream?

    _____

    _____

    _____

    _____

# STEP 3 → Living Your Dream

*I have learned that if one advances confidently
in the direction of his dreams,
and endeavors to live the life he has imagined,
he will meet with success unexpected in common hours.*
*—Henry David Thoreau*

In the past week you had the opportunity to refine your dreams, including your Life Dream. Now it's time to move confidently in the direction of those dreams. Even when the way is difficult, if you endeavor to live the life you've imagined, you will meet with success—often when you least expect it. It's one of the wonderful benefits of dreaming big.

Discovering > Refining > **LIVING** > Teaching > Encouraging

# Day 15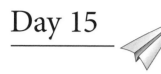

# **Trusting**
# Your Own
# **Judgment**

*A wise man makes his own decisions;*
*an ignorant man follows the public opinion.*
*Chinese Proverb*

## Overview

- *Step One: Do Your Homework*
- *Step Two: Seek Wise Counselors*
- *Step Three: Question Yourself*
- *Step Four: Act with Courage*

**As you seek to live your dream, will you follow public opinion or will you trust your own judgment?**

Jonas Salk, the inventor of polio vaccine, lived his dream—even in the face of criticism. In the process, he noticed a curious truth about his critics. "First," he said, "people will tell you that you are wrong. Then they will tell you that you are right, but what you're doing really isn't important. Finally, they will admit that you are right, and that what you're doing is very important . . . but after all, they knew it all the time." How will you develop confidence to stand-alone when you believe you are right?

> *There is a difference between conceit and confidence. Conceit is bragging about yourself. Confidence means you believe you can get the job done.*
>
> —Johnny Unitas

Accountants, attorneys, family, and friends are only advisors. They may think they have your best interests at heart. They may assume they know more about the feasibility of your dreams than you know yourself. *But they may be wrong.* The final decision as to whether any one of your dreams is realistic, or not, remains exclusively with you.

The further you get out of your own area of expertise, the more vulnerable you become. When you're an expert in a given area and your trustworthy outside counsel agrees with your perspective, go ahead and make a fast decision. But when you're in an area in which you know very little and you don't have an expert you really trust, take the following four steps to increase your knowledge. Knowledge leads to confidence and confidence gives courage.

## Step One: Do Your Homework

The first way to gain knowledge is by doing your own research. Fortunately, we have many excellent resources available to us today. Here are a few:

### Books

Books help us know ourselves and gain mastery in a particular area. If we didn't believe that, Paul and I wouldn't be writing this book. Even so, authors are not all knowing. Don't automatically assume that because information is in a book, it's right, wise, or applies to you. Look for what is true and strikes you as able to withstand the test of time. When the author's counsel does not take into account a situation like yours, trust your own judgment.

## The Internet

It is simply amazing the knowledge that can be gained from the Internet. We have whole libraries of information available to us in the convenience of our own homes. Unfortunately, almost anyone can pose as an expert on the Internet and claim to know all about a subject. Crackpots abound. To discern what is true, check the credentials and the track record of the "expert." It's easy to choose between the "expert" who says it won't fly . . . and the one who *has flown*.

> *Confidence is courage at ease.*
>
> —DANIEL MAHER

## Parents

Just at the turn of the twentieth century, Bishop Milton Wright was asked to make a judgment on one of the popular writings of the day that suggested humans might design and construct a machine that would make them airborne. The Bishop's statement was, "Only angels are meant to fly, and not a man!"

But it was near this same time that two young men, brothers in their thirties, thought the Bishop was wrong. They labored on a primitive machine at the sandy beach of Kitty Hawk, North Carolina. They brought a great faith to a very doubtful project because they believed that humans *could* fly.

The brothers' first attempts were futile; they didn't even get off the ground. But finally, on that lonely beach, the brothers proved they were right when their flying machine was airborne a total of 128 feet. Their names? Orville and Wilbur Wright, the famous sons of Bishop Milton Wright.[1]

Just because your parents are older and you respect and honor them doesn't mean automatically that they are smarter, wiser, or more right than you are. Some people who are older have had less experience than you in dreaming big. Your parents are not you. Even though you are younger, your perspective actually may be wiser. On the other hand, the counsel of your parents might be very wise. Consider what your parents say, but trust your own judgment.

**Friends**

In addition to our parents, all of us gain a lot of knowledge from our friends. They help to keep us informed. Trusted friends hold us accountable. Yet, when we ask them for advice, we must remember that no one knows what's inside us the way we do. A friend may listen only a minute to what you've been dreaming about for hours or even years. If they give *snap judgments* based on *snap assumptions*, it likely will lead to *snap poor advice!*

When you're listening to a friend in their area of expertise and the counsel doesn't make sense to you, *do not follow it blindly*. Ask the friend to clearly explain how they arrived at their conclusion. Listen. Then trust your own judgment.

## Step Two: Seek Wise Counselors

Think about the qualities you want in your advisors. You might jot down your list in the margins. Here are ten characteristics we look for in a wise counselor.

*The wise counselor tells the truth.*

You don't want people to play games with you. You need counselors who will be absolutely honest. This is hard for most of us because we tend to select friends (and counselors) who make us feel good about ourselves. We like to be complimented and supported. But we don't need little lies or untruths. We need truth spoken in love.

*The wise counselor has a consistent track record.*

Look at a person's background, career, and family life. You want someone who has shown consistent integrity in life and who will be consistent with you. If you seek financial advice or career counsel, look for an expert with a proven record in that field. As financial author, Dave Ramsey, says, "Don't take financial advice from broke people!"

*The wise counselor seeks the same kind of success you seek.*

That's critical. If you and your counselor have different goals, and different visions of what constitutes success, you'll wind up with bad advice. It's best to find someone who can share your values and your dream.

*The wise counselor has the knowledge you know you need.*

You're looking for someone to fill in the gaps of your knowledge. The natural tendency is to get close to people who share your knowledge base, avoiding people who are knowledgeable in ways you are not. You have to overcome those tendencies and seek people who are strong in areas you need to know.

*The wise counselor really cares about you.*

You want somebody who has *your* best interests at heart. You want someone who will stand by your side during the tough times. Those counselors are hard to find, but they're worth their weight in gold.

*The wise counselor is willing to understand your personality.*

Each of us has quirks and idiosyncrasies. That's what makes us interesting . . . and sometimes frustrating. A good counselor understands your personality and is willing to help you.

*The wise counselor is practical, flexible, and filled with common sense.*
Good counselors won't get carried away by idealism. They have their feet on the ground. You need common sense to steer you away from frivolous endeavors and refocus you in productive, realistic directions.

*The wise counselor has a positive outlook.*
You need someone who looks at your dream with optimism. Someone consistently negative will make a poor counselor.

*The wise counselor knows when to keep his or her mouth shut.*
Good counselors don't gossip. They don't betray your trust. They don't leak confidential information to other people.

*The wise counselor has an awesome respect for God.*
There is a proverb that puts it this way: "The fear of the Lord is the beginning of knowledge."[2] For centuries man has known that you cannot build an enduring culture on a self-centered foundation. If man is at the center, self-interest becomes inevitable and decay follows. A wise counselor has the courage to tell you when you have dreams that run counter to wisdom.

## Step Three: Question Yourself

When following your own dreams, you may come to a point where even the men and women whose judgment you've trusted the most are not able to help. They can't give you an accurate perspective on the dream in your heart. To gain discernment, you need to ask yourselves a few profound questions.

1.  At its essence, in one sentence, what decision am I facing now as I move toward my dreams? What is the "bottom-bottom" line? If I can identify that decision, I can manage it.

2.  Have I given myself twenty-four hours to let this decision settle in my mind? Am I thinking about this decision with

a clear head, or am I too fatigued to be making major decisions? How do I really feel about this decision and its potential to help me get to my dreams? What questions linger unresolved in my mind? Is this decision integrated with my life "center?"

3. What would happen if I decide YES to this decision? And NO? How would this affect my overall dream strategy?

4. What difference will this decision make 5, 10, 50, and 100 years from now?

5. What key assumptions am I making related to cost, time commitments, and benefits? Are they accurate?

6. How do my daily decisions affect my overall master plan? Which get me off track? Which speed me along the way toward my dreams?

7. Should I seek outside counsel on this decision? How would each of my top three most respected counselors advise me? How do my spouse and family feel about this decision? How are they affected by it?

8. Can the big decision be broken into sub-parts and lower risk decisions made at a few "go / no go" points along the way?

9. What long-term solutions will move me closer to my dreams?

10. Is this the best timing? Why or why not? If not now, when?

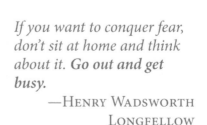

*If you want to conquer fear, don't sit at home and think about it.* **Go out and get busy.**

—Henry Wadsworth Longfellow

When you believe you have adequate knowledge, don't wait until you know everything. It's time to act with confidence.

## Step Four: Act with Courage

How do you develop the courage to stand alone and trust your judgment? Where does a great leader, like Dr. Martin Luther King, Jr., get his inner strength to overcome fears and face life-threatening situations? Here's Dr. King's answer.

> *I sat there and thought about a beautiful little daughter who had just been born . . . She was the darling of my life. I'd come in night after night and see that little gentle smile. And I sat at that table thinking about that little girl and thinking about the fact that she could be taken from me any minute.*
>
> *And I started thinking about a dedicated, devoted and loyal wife who was over there asleep. And she could be taken from me, or I could be taken from her. And I got to the point that I couldn't take it any longer. I was weak. Something said to me, you can't call on Daddy now; he's up in Atlanta a hundred and seventy-five miles away. You can't even call on Mama now. You've got to call on that something in that person your Daddy used to tell you about, that power that can make a way out of no way.*
>
> *And I discovered then that religion had to become real to me, and I had to know God for myself. And I bowed down over that cup of coffee. I never will forget it . . . I prayed a prayer, and I prayed out loud that night. I said, "Lord, I'm down here trying to do what's right. I think I'm right. I think the cause that we represent is right. But Lord, I must confess that I'm weak now. I'm faltering. I'm losing my courage. And I can't let the people see me like this because if they see me weak and losing my courage, they will begin to get weak . . . "*
>
> *And it seemed at that moment that I could hear an inner voice saying to me, "Martin Luther, stand up for righteousness.*

*Stand up for justice. Stand up for truth. And lo I will be with you, even until the end of the world"* . . . *I heard the voice of Jesus saying still to fight on. He promised never to leave me, never to leave me alone. No never alone, no never alone. He promised never to leave, never to leave me alone . . . Almost at once my fears began to go. My uncertainty disappeared.*[3]

When you have times of uncertainty, focus your attention on what you know for sure. Then act with courage. Believe you can get the job done against the rush of critics and fears. Choose to trust your own judgment.

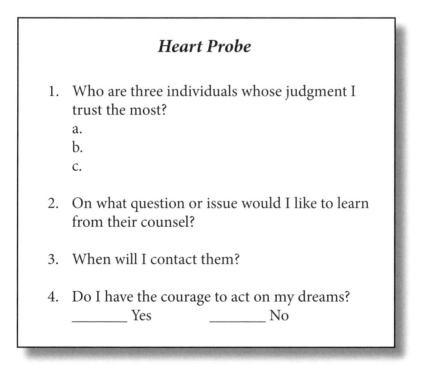

### *Heart Probe*

1. Who are three individuals whose judgment I trust the most?
   a.
   b.
   c.

2. On what question or issue would I like to learn from their counsel?

3. When will I contact them?

4. Do I have the courage to act on my dreams?
   _____ Yes _____ No

# Day 16

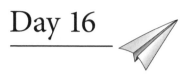

# Protecting
# **Your Dreams**

*I am determined not to allow anyone
to steal my dreams.[1]*
—*Dexter R. Yager, Sr.*

## Overview

- *Protect Your Dreams in the Formative Stages*
- *Do a Reality Check So Others Won't Have To*
- *Properly Identify the Source of Negative Pressure*

**In the early stages, your dream is about as vulnerable as a soap bubble in a high wind along jagged rock cliffs.**

Big dreams can be so exciting that you want to talk about them to anyone who will listen. Unfortunately, sometimes you may end up telling the wrong person—someone who enjoys poking holes in your "bubble."

## Protect Your Dreams . . . especially in the Formative Stages

You will need to protect your dream in four basic areas:

## Emotionally

Some people may seem supportive, but they ask too many heavy questions too early in the process. They may not be trying to make you look foolish, but at the end of the conversation you may feel that you haven't considered the most important things and that the dream probably won't work out after all.

Avoid people who don't meet the standards for wise counsel we discussed in Chapter 15. Later on you may want to run your idea past some pessimists to make sure that you can answer their basic questions *to your satisfaction.* But remember to trust your own judgment. Look for cheerleaders for your dream . . . or you may be grilled by Monday-morning-quarterbacks who have never played the game.

## Financially

Sometimes a dream takes skills you may not yet possess, such as financial analysis and projections. In that case, you need the help of others who can serve as your financial advisers. It works best if you choose two to four people you know and trust; people who know what you are doing and want to see you win.

You will need to share with these advisors confidential financial information along with your Dream Strategy Plan. To benefit you, they must have proven track records of managing their own lives and organizations profitably. These people serve as an invaluable resource and an objective sounding board for the development of your dreams.

## Legally

You may meet with an attorney to discuss a building project or an enterprise you'd like to start, only to have the attorney say to you it's not legally feasible. But if you know it is not immoral or unethical, seriously consider the possibility of getting the laws changed. You don't want to break the law, but don't assume that the law is automatically right and cannot be rewritten, amended, or waived to accommodate your dream.

**Socially**

In the early stages of your dream you need to put up a protective barrier against negative peer pressure. There are relatively few people in society who have the ability to stay with their dream when all their friends say it won't work. You can be one of the few.

People may laugh at you. Ignore the laughter or let it motivate you to prove them wrong. Ask yourself, "Who is the primary audience for my dream? Who am I trying to help?" As long as your primary audience gets the service, help, information, or material you want to give them, what does it matter what other people say?

Because your dreams in the beginning may be as fragile as an infant, protect them like a father or mother protecting their children. Develop a fierce courage to defend your dream from all potential dream stealers. Imagine yourself a mother bear protecting her cubs. Then nurse your dreams to strength and maturity.

## Do a Reality Check So Others Won't Have To

*How realistic are your dreams?*

Who has achieved dreams similar to yours? What can you learn from them? What obstacles did they face? How did they overcome them? What time frame did it take for them to achieve their dreams?

*What would your three most trusted advisors say?*

Advisors you trust can sharpen your focus. But remember— even trusted advisors can lack certain information, make unwarranted assumptions, and have perspectives that cause them to give unwise council. They might say without adequate thought, "That's unrealistic!"—meaning it would be unrealistic for them. They are not taking into account that you are not bound by their limits. No one knows you and your dreams like you do.

> *The best way to protect your dream is to fortify the foundation it's built on.*
> —BEN ROBERTS

*How does your dream measure up in four essential categories?* Answering the questions in each category will help you fortify the foundation of your dreams.

### A. Time–Planning

Is it realistic to do what you want to do in the time you have? Does your plan take into account the time you think you will need?

### B. Energy–People

Is it physically possible for you to do what you would like to do? If not, could you put a team together over the next ten years to accomplish your dream?

### C. Money–Capital

How could you fund your dream? Will you need to take out a loan? How do you plan to repay the loan? What could you do to generate an additional income stream?

### D. Tools–Resources

What tools do you need to get the job done? Do you have these tools? If not, where are they available? Do you know how to use the resources available to you? If not, do you have someone who can teach you? Don't underestimate the value of a tool. In many situations tools make the difference whether or not a dream is realistic.

# Properly Identify the Source of Negative Pressure

I remember a friend who came to me one day absolutely exasperated, fearful, and panicked. Yes, it was that bad . . . or so it seemed to him. He said, "Bobb, everything in my life is falling apart. What am I going to do?"

Sensing my friend was overreacting to an imbalance in his life, I suggested he take ten minutes to do the following exercise. You may want to do it as well.

1. Write out everything that's weighing heavily on your shoulders today.
2. Divide that list of things into the eight categories of the Dream Balance Chart.
   o Family—your immediate and extended family
   o Financial—your money, investments, and debt concerns
   o Vocational—your career or work activity
   o Social—your friends, social clubs, civic activities
   o Spiritual—your relationship with God
   o Mental—your reading, learning, and personal growth goals
   o Emotional—your feelings of love, anger, hope, anxiety, confidence, etc.
   o Physical—your exercise, nutrition, recreation.
3. Add a list of all the things that are going right in your life.

After completing this exercise, my friend came back with sort of a sheepish grin on his face. "You know, the more I looked at it, the more I could see I'm under severe financial pressure right now, but actually things are going well in the other areas of my life."

Generalized anxiety can overwhelm your dreams. But when you identify the pressure points, you are better able to get a grip on your dreams, to evaluate the pressures, and to begin to solve problems. Knowing the source of negative pressures helps to make life manageable and prevents you from allowing anyone to steal your Life Dream.

## *Heart Probe*

1. Who or what could steal my Life Dream if I fail to protect it?


2. As I review this chapter, what specific steps will I take to protect my dream?

# Day 17

# **Overcoming**
## Dismissal,
## Divorce, or
## Despair

*Think of me as a fellow-patient in the same hospital who, having been admitted a little earlier, could give some advice.*
—C. S. Lewis

## Overview

- *Rest*
- *Renew*
- *Restore*

### Life is not all that it should be.

You may be in your prime and suddenly out of work. You may desire to give happiness, security, and love to family members, but your best attempts are rebuffed. Your life may look ideal on the outside, but deep in your secret core are unfilled longings that lead to despair. You may be ready for a break down . . . or *a break through.*

When our personal world is broken, our emotional landscape feels like the aftermath of a hurricane. All the pieces that would normally fit within clear boundaries are strewn all over. There seem to be no protective walls, no barriers against unwanted experience, no predictability. We feel vulnerable to psychological looters. Fears escalate.

When fear increases, confidence in our dreams decreases. There may be even a fear of dreaming, a fear of "getting one's hopes up," of counting on something, of trusting anyone because our dreams now seem utterly impossible. Everything inside signals break-down.

Although each one of us is unique and no one's suffering is exactly like the pain of another, *healing is possible*. There are enough fellow-patients in "the hospital of life" from whom we can gain wisdom. One such fellow-patient is King David. With remarkable candor, he shares from his own experience three ways his brokenness was overcome.

> *He makes me lie down in green pastures,*
> *He leads me beside the still waters,*
> *He restores my soul.*[1]

As a youth, David was a shepherd. Now as the anointed king of Israel, David was viewed by the people as their "shepherd-king," a widely used metaphor for kings in the ancient Near East and in Israel. But David views God as his Shepherd-King. He acknowledges that, like sheep, he cannot do much for himself. Notice it is the Shepherd who initiates help in the midst of David's adversity.

David used the image of sheep for himself even though it's not complimentary. He shows us his heart—without pretense, without defense, without any attempt to impress. He simply is being real. Real brokenness makes truth easier to tell.

Rest, renewal, and restoration highlight David's story. In the midst of our adversity, these three principles can help us overcome the brokenness we sometimes experience.

> *Adversity is the first path to truth.*
> —LORD BYRON

## Rest

*He makes me lie down.*

Sheep don't like to lie down and rest quietly because of a natural timidity. Things have to be just right for them to lie down naturally. They have to feel *free* to rest.

- Free from fear
- Free from annoyances, like flies and other pests
- Free from hunger, tension, and danger.

Because sheep do not naturally feel such freedom, the shepherd *makes* the sheep lie down. If he is a good shepherd, the sheep learn to trust his presence and obey his command to rest. For David, his good shepherd was the *Shepherd*. The presence of God in his life enabled him to rest.

During our break-down points, it's difficult to know how much rest we need. Typically eight hours of good sleep gives us the feeling of being rested and ready to return to the tasks at hand. However, when we are in a state of emotional trauma, such as a death or divorce, we may go into a state of "deep fatigue." We wake up after eight or even ten hours sleep and we're still as tired as we were when we went to bed.

If deep fatigue describes you now and you have lost the ability to dream temporarily, don't worry about your dreams. Concentrate on a season of deep rest—the "deep rest" your soul needs. "Deep rest" is when you do nothing you don't have to do. You sleep as much as you can possibly sleep; you rest as much as you can rest.

Answer this question: "Now, this hour, today, what can I depend on? Who can I trust?" Bottom line: soul fatigue requires deep rest. Deep rest requires the healing presence of the Good Shepherd. Whatever you've believed about God in the past is not the issue now. Simply ask God to release you from your fears. Let the force of His goodness make you lie down.

## Renew

*He leads me beside quiet waters.*

Because sheep have a tendency to be skittish, rushing water does not calm them. When everything around us is chaotic, we need the *quiet waters*. This quiet water is not stagnant or contaminated; it's pure and refreshing. It's not dangerous; it's calming, like early morning fishing with a loving Papa on a quiet lake.

Where can we get this "quiet water?" Sheep don't have a keen awareness of where they are and where they need to go. They're vulnerable to blindly following other sheep—and getting terribly lost. In some ways they mirror us, which is why David used the analogy. We need to follow a leader who has been down the path we are going; one who knows how to get us safely to our destination. We need to be *led* by the Shepherd.

When brokenness occurs, we may not know which way to go. We are vulnerable to following the crowd and getting stuck in counterproductive patterns. What we need is transformation from the inside out.

According to the Apostle Paul, *renewing* our mind leads to transformation. "*Do not conform any longer to the pattern of this world, but be transformed by the renewing of your mind.*"[2] Renewal results from a fresh understanding of what God has done for those who believe in Him.

## Restore

*He restores my soul.*

As David reflects on his depression, he asks himself, "*Why are you downcast, O my soul? Why so disturbed within me?*"[3] In this context, the word "soul" refers to one's self—a living, conscious, personal core—one's whole being. During times of crisis, our souls feel as if they are *cast down*, like a sheep.

Phillip Keller, a shepherd himself, says that when sheep are "cast," they have somehow rolled onto their backs and cannot get up. Their legs move frantically, but they are helpless. Even normally healthy sheep can be cast, brought down by the weight of their own wool or by the lay of the land. Try as they might, they are doomed to die without the help of a shepherd.[4]

To be restored is to be put back on our feet. We may stubbornly resist help. We may be too embarrassed to ask for help. We may believe we can handle it on our own. But when we are "cast," we have no choice. Repeatedly King David asked himself, "Why are you cast down, O my soul?" Finally he was convinced of the only adequate solution to his miserable condition. "Put your hope in God." For David, ultimately there was no one to turn to but the Shepherd who alone could restore his soul.

> *God uses the pain of shattered dreams to help us discover our desire for God, to help us begin dreaming the highest dream.*[5]
> —LARRY CRABB

The stimulus is pain, heartache, brokenness. The natural response is break-down. But there is another choice. We can choose to allow pain to bring us to a point of healing, of overcoming. When we are restored, we can start dreaming again—higher, bigger, and more balanced than before.

---

### *Heart Probe*

1. Realistically, what is my greatest need at this point?
   - ❏ Rest
   - ❏ Renew
   - ❏ Restore

2. What people, books, and other resources can be of help to me?

3. How would I describe my relationship to the Shepherd? What can I do today to strengthen that relationship?

---

# Day 18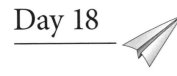

# Facing Unexpected
# **Realities**

*In a manner contrary to weak reactions,*
*which immobilize the person and paralyze thought,*
*strong reactions stimulate motive energy*
*and open the sluice-gates of the imagination and the intellect*
*to an abundant flood of apt mental pictures,*
*interesting concepts, and pertinent arguments.*[1]
*—Paul Tournier, Swiss Psychotherapist*

## Overview

- *Illness*
- *Unemployment*
- *Fatigue*
- *Restrictions*
- *Mutiny*

**Reality can hurt.**

How do you react to life's bruises? Often without warning,
events happen that require us to respond. If we choose weak
reactions, we withdraw or become passive. Dreams diminish. If
we choose to react with strength, we rise to the occasion. Dreams
flourish.

Although we cannot predict with certainty what each of us will face, it does help to review a few common interruptions of our normal routines and determine ahead of time how we will respond. This chapter assists you in finding ways to approach five possible challenges with strength.

## Illness

Your friend has an exciting dream, but his wife has developed a severe health problem. The reality is that he is not able to pursue his dream at the level he could if his wife were healthy. When he seeks your counsel, ask him, "What is the most valuable use of your time right now?" The answer is clear. His love for his wife makes it the wise choice to focus his attention on her, even if it means putting the dream on hold for a period of time. Wouldn't you do the same?

## Unemployment

Boss Dillard knock knocks on your office door. You ask, "Who's there?" He replies, "Not you anymore." Layoffs can happen with little warning. Downsizing and corporate buyouts affect millions every year. Unless you have a very healthy severance package or a large savings account, what will you do? Should you seek another job in your field? Is it time to branch out into another field of work? What preparations do you need to include in your Strategic Plan? Will you begin your own business? How can you keep your dream in focus?

## Fatigue

You're overworked. Your job requires more and more of your time, and your responsibilities at home seem endless. As you assess your situation, you can't imagine having the energy to pursue your dream.

Perhaps it's time to do a brutally honest self-assessment. Do you need to find a job that is less demanding? Can you request a lateral change within your company that would ease the stress? When did you have your last physical? Do you have a vitamin deficiency that supplements could correct? Are you careful about what you eat? Are you getting adequate exercise? What on your "To Do" list can you eliminate? What responsibilities can you delegate? What is the wisest decision you could make given your circumstances?

Although dreaming *takes* a certain amount of energy, it also *gives* energy back. I find it's highly productive to set aside one workday out of twenty per month (5 percent) for brainstorming about my dreams. When I do, the remaining 95 percent of my work time is more productive. What changes can you make to fight fatigue with more energy?

## Restrictions

Your employer has a "no moonlighting" demand in the company policy. You feel the company controls not only your work time, but your personal time as well. You begin to resent your employer for keeping you from pursuing your dream.

A hostile dependency relationship can be a very stressful reality. Ask yourself some serious questions: "Do I need to find another job?" "Is there a way to pursue the dream and still stay within the rules of the company?" Take the initiative. See if you can reach an agreement with your employer. If not, determine how long you want to stay in a situation that pays your bills, but denies your personal freedom.

## Mutiny

What if your spouse has a dream that's not parallel to yours? What if you're moving forward on the same ship, working together to keep it afloat, but wanting to go in different directions?

Aim to sincerely build *teamwork* with your spouse in every other area of your life together. You may have to pursue your dream without the support of your spouse. In any case, affirm marital oneness as your higher priority. Don't let a dream come between you. Do all you can to enhance your marriage and support your partner's dream. Let the strength of your dream and the positive affect it has on you win his/her support.

Reality can be brutal. Most often there are no easy answers. But in Chapter Eight we learned that between a stimulus and a response is our *freedom to choose.*

> *There's bound to be rough waters*
> *And I know I'll take some falls*
> *But with the good Lord as my*
> *captain, I can make it through*
> *them all . . .*
> —GARTH BROOKS, *The River*

When you face unexpected realities, you have the freedom to respond with strength. We coach you to choose wisely.

---

### *Heart Probe*

1. What unexpected realities am I facing right now?

2. Would I honestly characterize my reactions to these realities as strong or weak?

3. What decisions can I make that would enable me to move toward my dreams with strength?

# Day 19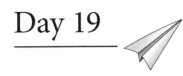

# Dreaming **Breakout** Dreams

*Oh that you would bless me and enlarge my territory!*
*Let your hand be with me, and keep me*
*from harm so that I will be free from pain.[1]*
*—The Prayer of Jabez*

## Overview

- *If I Were Your Paid Consultant*
- *Survival, Success, and Significance*
- *Progressing Beyond Success to Significance*

### Jabez dreamed big.

Jabez wanted the blessing of God, an enlarged territory, a greater measure of influence. In the process, he did not want to get hurt or suffer the pain of hurting someone else. In something of an understatement, the writer of Chronicles reports, "And God granted his request."[2]

Like Jabez, you may be praying for an opportunity to expand your territory. What does dreaming big mean in your life? If you sat down with a trusted friend and felt free to explore the breadth of your vision for your life, what would be included? What counsel would you want?

For over thirty years now I have made a living consulting as an executive mentor in the areas of personal and organization development. Basically, I help people decide where they are and where they want to go and I help them get there in their time frame. If I were your consultant, we would also begin where you are in life right now.

> *Do all the good you can, by all the means you can, in all the places you can, to all the people you can, as long as ever you can.*
> —JOHN WESLEY

## If I Were Your Paid Consultant

If you and I could sit down with a cup of coffee and discuss where you are in life today, the following chart will show you the type of counsel I would more than likely give you. My counsel would depend on your dream, your confidence, and your level of responsibility.

| BASIC SITUATION | POSSIBLE OPTIONS |
|---|---|
| **A.** *I've Outgrown My Dream* | 1. Take a retreat with *Dreaming Big*—rethink your life dream and how to take it to the next level |
| | 2. Examine the lives and actions of others who are doing what you are doing on a much larger scale |
| | 3. Arrange some time with some peers whose enterprises are at least 50 percent larger than yours. Use them as a sounding board, an advisory council. Ask them, "Where would you recommend I go from here?" |
| | 4. Attend a convention in your area of interest where your dreams can be expanded. |
| | 5. Ask your mentor for input and perspective. |
| | 6. Be aware that you may be vulnerable to someone criticizing your dream. Don't give up your dream. Act slowly. Review what you are passionate about. |

| BASIC SITUATION | POSSIBLE OPTIONS |
|---|---|
| **B.**<br>*I've Outgrown My Confidence* | 7. Concentrate on restoring the predictable parts of your life and work situation.<br><br>8. Get some "deep rest." Remember as Vince Lombardi said, "Fatigue makes cowards of us all."<br><br>9. Get some time with your "cheer leaders."<br><br>10. Take a few days away—to get a renewed perspective; to regain your big picture; to review your plans.<br><br>11. Ponder your top 3 measurable priorities/goals/problems/opportunities for the next 90 days.<br><br>12. Review your positive progress list.<br><br>13. Seek an objective perspective from your mentor, consultant, close friend, etc.<br><br>14. Is it possible that you have taken on too many outside responsibilities? Perhaps if you were to resign from a few activities, your dream would seem more possible. |
| **C.**<br>*I've Outgrown My Position,* **or** *Organization* | 15. Be aware that you may be vulnerable to a new career position that would turn out to be far less suitable to you.<br><br>16. Have an honest discussion with your team leader or mentor about seeking broader responsibilities.<br><br>17. Hold a "dream sparking" retreat with your team. Dream about how your organization could double or triple in the next year thus enlarging your responsibilities. |

Caution—we don't intend for you to take all the actions on these lists. Simply pick one or two that make a lot of sense to you at this point and consider them.

## Survival, Success, and Significance

Right now, where is the current hub of your time, energy, and money? Are you focused on surviving, succeeding, or making a significant difference in other people's lives? In the following chart, notice the *differences in perspective* during the survival, success, and significance phases of life. Circle the box that reflects where you are now even if it does not correspond directly with your values or where you'd like to be.

|  | **SURVIVAL** | **SUCCESS** | **SIGNIFICANCE** |
|---|---|---|---|
| **FOCUS** | Self—i.e. keep from drowning yourself | Self—i.e. winning more and more swim meets | Others—i.e. keeping someone else from drowning, helping another win a race. |
| **QUESTION** | Can we pay the bills? Can I keep my job? | How big can we get? | What difference can we make? |
| **ORIENTATION** | Threats—getting beyond day-to-day "hand to mouth" survival. | Priorities—accumulating more profit. | Dreams—making a significant difference. |
| **OPENNESS TO NEW IDEAS** | Low | Medium | High |
| **OPENNESS TO GIVING** | Low | Medium | High |
| **TIME FRAME** | Immediate | 1–2 Years | 5–100 Years |
| **ENERGY** | Forced Energy | Driven Energy | Dream Energy |
| **MODE** | Reactive | Proactive | Proactive |

In reality, we move back and forth between survival, success, and significance. For example, we may feel like we want to make a significant difference . . . but then we get home and find the water pipes have burst and the house is a mess and we're back into the "How do we survive this situation?" mode. Dreaming big pulls us through our temporary setbacks. It keeps us moving long term toward significance.

## Progressing Beyond Success to Significance

What do you want your legacy to be? Most likely you want to make a difference. You want to come to the end of your life feeling that many lives were better because you were here—your life, the lives of your children, the lives of people on your team, the lives of countless people you have met through the years.

Whatever area you choose to impact or influence, do you want to leave it better than you found it? Do you want to expand the territory of your influence? If so, you're dreaming big!

> **DREAMING BIG**
>
> *One of the reasons we bought the Magic was to expand the opportunity to share our values with our players, the Orlando community, and the world at large. We wanted to have a positive impact on all those people.*
>
> —RICH DEVOS
> OWNER OF THE
> ORLANDO MAGIC

## *Heart Probe*

1.  If I am discouraged, what do I think is the reason?
    - ❏ Have I outgrown my dream?
    - ❏ Have I outgrown my confidence?
    - ❏ Have I outgrown my responsibilities?
    - ❏ Other _____

2.  Am I focused now on:
    - ❏ Survival?
    - ❏ Success?
    - ❏ Significance?

3.  Where do I want to be focused?

# Day 20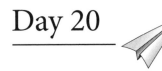

# Enjoying What **Matters** Most

*No matter what happens in life,
a wonderful dream is available, always, that if pursued
will generate an unfamiliar, radically new experience.
That experience, strange at first,
will eventually be recognized as joy.*[1]
—*Larry Crabb*

## Overview

- *Where is Your Focus*
- *The Downside of Feeling Driven by the Past*
- *The Upside of Being Pulled into the Future*
- *Experiencing the Joy*

### Does your Life Dream give you joy?

People who focus only on day-to-day activities frequently look back at the end of the year and ask themselves, "What did I really get done? What did I really do? Did I make any difference? Did I just get my 'To Do' list done?"

Think back over the last thirty to ninety days. Now answer this one question: "In this time period, where has my focus been?"

Have you been focused in the:
- **Past**—trying to prove something to someone or dealing with a phobic fear from the past or re-doing something that happened in the past?
- **Present**—living day-to-day, plodding, making it happen, getting it done?
- **Future**—feeling you're being pulled forward by your dreams?

Over the years, we've observed hundreds of top-level men and women in a wide variety of professions, ministries, enterprises, and projects. Some have been driven by phobias from the past while others are constantly focused by their Life Dream. The differences are quite amazing.

Those energized by the future don't get stuck in melancholy doldrums about the past, nor do they experience the mediocre plodding of the day-to-day grind. Their focus on the future and the progress they are making toward their dreams generates a radically new experience they eventually recognize as joy. What about you?

## Where is Your Focus?

Circle or highlight the boxes that describe you at this time.

| Focus | Past Fears | Present Survival | Future Vision |
|---|---|---|---|
| Frequently Feel | pushed by the past | stagnant | pulled by a life dream |
| Source of Energy | phobic fear coming from childhood | current project | ideas, priorities, dreams |
| Motivation Model | whipped | on a treadmill | chasing a carrot |
| Feel in Control | no | no / yes | yes |
| Effect on the Human System | negative, unhealthy | neutral | positive, healthy |
| Projects | lots of activity, little holistic focus | moderate activity, little holistic focus | lots of activity, clear holistic focus |
| Feeling of Significance and Contribution | low | low | high |
| Energy Level | high | sometimes high, sometimes low | high |

114

# The Downside of Feeling Driven by the Past

I'll never forget a 2:00 a.m. conversation with one of my lifelong friends, King Crow, president of the Arkansas Federal Savings Bank. We were discussing the drivenness we'd seen in executives. We agreed the following story captured the feeling of being driven by the past.

Imagine for a minute a tall mountain, maybe ten thousand feet high. Around this cone-shaped mountain there is an eight-foot, one-lane road that winds from the bottom of the mountain clear to the top. It's just big enough for one car to go on. It's a very steep mountain. If at any time you happened to fall off the road, for whatever reason, you'd drop hundreds of feet to your destruction.

You're walking up the road alone with the goal of reaching the top. You're making progress, but it's a tall mountain, and very steep. It is going to take you a long time, maybe years. You work hard, you walk, you jog up the mountain until you're just exhausted. You lie down and go to sleep.

A few hours later you wake up to the sound of a bulldozer—a huge bulldozer, an earthmover. It's coming up the mountain behind you at a fairly slow pace. You get up and keep ahead of it. You run and get ahead of it. But it keeps moving all night and all day. It goes twenty-four hours a day, seven days a week. It doesn't have a driver. It's on an automatic track of some kind. It keeps coming at you, no matter how you talk to it, no matter what you say to it. It just keeps coming at you. If you sat down on the road for just a little bit and didn't move, its angled plow blade would push you right off the mountain to your destruction.

You work as hard as you can all day long. You go to sleep and rest. Again, you wake up to the sound of the bulldozer. It's only three feet from your head. You jump up startled and sprint ahead a quarter mile. Then you run a half-mile ahead. By the end of the day you think, "I'm far enough ahead of that thing. I'd better go to sleep." You go to sleep, but the next morning it's on you again.

Frequently people who have a sense of *drivenness* don't even know what the bulldozer represents, what is *driving* them. They don't know whether it's a fear of failure, a fear of rejection, or a fear of something else. So they try everything to escape the "dozer." They get involved in ten times too many things. They don't even know what they want to be or do or accomplish or get or borrow or buy or have or own. There's just an endless trying, with rare satisfaction, to get to some point where they feel like that bulldozer isn't chasing them anymore.

Do you feel like a bulldozer is after you? Do you feel as if you are out of control and you can't quit? If you feel driven, what is driving you? What from your past causes you to try to prove something or to accomplish something?

We suggest that *drivenness* often results from phobic fears that have their origin in our childhood.[2] Phobias do create a form of energy in us—high energy driving us to stay ahead of the bulldozer of rejection, failure, and all those things that push us and push us and push us up the mountain. But the whole process is negative and unhealthy. It's *being driven* by the past rather than *being pulled* by the future.

If you live with high activity and have fears of low contribution, you're going to feel exhausted, used, burned up, and spent. Activity without a Life Dream leads to hundreds of pieces with no sense of the whole. There's no sense of charging your battery, of refueling your engines. Your energy is taken from you, and not given back to you. The bulldozer forces you to run, but it doesn't give you any new fuel to run on. Exhausting.

## The Upside of Being Pulled into the Future

On the other hand, when you have *dream energy*, you have a positive, healthy energy for the future. You have a far greater feeling of control. Think of a ski tow rope. You grab onto the rope, and it pulls you up the mountain. When you get as high up the mountain as you want, you just let go. Then you turn around and ski back down. If you want to go up a hundred yards and ski down, you can. If you want to go up five hundred yards and ski down, you can. You are in total control of where you stop based on your own comfort level.

Your Life Dream gives you a future focus. It gets you out of bed each morning eager to face a new day. It invites you, attracts you, pulls you to move forward and make a difference.

Recently I was driving around the Lake Wylie, South Carolina, area. I pulled off to the side of an undeveloped piece of property. There was a bulldozer on the land, and some trees were knocked down. A lot of mud. Looked awful. But somebody saw its future potential . . . beautiful.

## Experiencing the Joy

Realistically, we live each day partly focused on the past, partly focused on the present, and partly focused on the future. So you may ask, "What's the big deal?"

The mountains you face are the big deal. Life has its heartaches and suffering. If you do not have an adequate view of the future, your mountains of trouble will rob you of joy.

Will just dreaming about the future turn gloom into happiness? Of course not. But deciding where to focus your primary energy will affect a lot of what you become, have, do, or contribute. If you want to be more future focused, you will find it helpful to forget past negative hurts and focus on your future positive dreams to energize you today.

---

### *Heart Probe*

1. Where has my thinking and motivation been focused?
   - ❑ The past
   - ❑ The present
   - ❑ The future

2. If I am not as future focused as I want to be, what changes will help me live my Life Dream?

---

# Day 21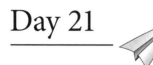

# Mentoring the **Next** Generation

> *It is one of the most beautiful compensations*
> *of this life that no man can sincerely help another*
> *without helping himself.*
> *—Ralph Waldo Emerson*

## Overview
- *What is Mentoring?*
- *What is an Ideal Protégé?*

### How would you describe your passion in life?

Bob Buford, president of a successful cable television company, founder of Leadership Network, and author of the book *Half Time*, is a friend I've known for a number of years. Not long ago, Bob asked me one of his "zinger" questions. "Bobb, how would you describe your passion today?" Without hesitation my response was "MENTORING!" It's part of my Life Dream.

We include this chapter in *Dreaming Big* because mentoring is probably part of what it will mean for you to *live your dream*. Can you imagine how fulfilling a mentoring relationship can be? Think of the emotion you felt when you achieved something important to you—dating the person of your dreams, making the team, earning your degree, winning a prize, getting married, hearing your two year old son say, "Mommy, I wuv you." Likely you will feel a similar emotion when you help others achieve what is important to them. It's one of the "beautiful compensations of life."

## What is Mentoring?

*Ideally, mentoring is a lifelong relationship in which a mentor helps a protégé reach her/his full potential.*

Mentoring is my passion. Why? The answer is written clearly on the faces of those I have mentored. There is intense satisfaction seeing the countenance of another person light up with joy when my mentoring helped them succeed. Most often my mentoring is in the context of vocational dreams and visions. But mentoring also affects every other aspect of life—spiritual, mental, social, athletic, etc. I realize that the world we know today is a reflection of the cumulative dreams of our ancestors. The world our children will know will be in a significant way a reflection of our mentoring. Wow!

Any person who is younger or less experienced than you could benefit from you handing off what you know to them. Although you as the mentor assume a responsibility for your protégé, you can relax in the relationship because you share what you know. When you meet with your protégé, simply ask them two mentoring questions: *"What are your priorities?"* and *"How can I help?"* Then enjoy mentoring the next generation.[2]

> **DREAMING BIG**
> *Our mission is to mobilize and train one million adults by the year 2015 to shape the next generation of leaders.*[1]
> —JEFF MYERS
> PASSING THE BATON INTL.

# What is an Ideal Protégé?

A protégé is a person with less experience than you who wants your help. If your dream includes helping people learn something, it's helpful to ask, "What do I look for in a protégé?" The following checklist is designed to help you answer that question. Before you choose one or more protégés, check to see if they have some or all of these qualities.

1.  **Easy to Believe In**
    Your ability to believe in a protégé is important. Ask yourself, "Do I believe this person is someone in whom I want to invest my energy and time? Do I believe in his/her potential?"

    You may spot a protégé whom you feel will someday provide leadership for your church, state, or nation. You may think this person will go far beyond your abilities in life. That's exciting. If the protégé looks up to you and is eager to learn from you, you could play a significant role in launching and expanding his or her influence.

2.  **Easy to Spend Time With**
    Look for someone you like naturally and enjoy being with both formally and informally. You want the feeling to be, "I like being with this person" . . . not "I should do this." This is a person with whom time seems to fly . . . not drag.

    It is interesting to note that some mentors respond far better to protégés of certain backgrounds. You may find yourself naturally drawn to troubled children, unwed mothers, people with special challenges—mental, emotional, physical, or of various other kinds. One of the most important things you can do is simply check with your own heart to see for what kind of person God has given you a special warmth, a special care, a special love, or a special compassion.

3.  **Easy to Keep Helping**
    In a mentor-protégé relationship, the mentor is typically more "other centered" than the protégé. The protégé often

forgets to say, "Thank you." He or she may be too caught up in their own insecurities and concerns to remember even basic courtesies. If there is very little emotional reward coming from the protégé, do you care enough about the protégé to continue giving without receiving a lot of personal appreciation?

4.  **Like Family**
    Make a heart commitment to be a friend for the long term. Grab on and hold on to this young person even when things don't go so well. Choose someone you can imagine yourself committed to helping even when he or she has melt-downs or failures.

5.  **Is Teachable**
    Is the potential protégé eager to learn from you? If your protégé is teachable, your natural energy level and interest in helping her toward her full potential will be high. If, on the other hand, she seems resistive or unteachable, your interest in continuing to mentor her over time will be drastically reduced.

6.  **One Who Respects You**
    Do you sense a natural respect and admiration for you from the protégé? If so, chances are he will be an eager student.

7.  **Self-Motivated**
    Will the protégé take the initiative in seeking you out and following through, or will you have to constantly prop him up, cheer him on, or get him out of a depression? What you are looking for, ideally, is a protégé who is self-motivated, one who will consistently seek you out, take the next step, want to grow, want to learn, want to stretch, and want to reach his full maturity.

8.  **A Comfortable Relationship**
    If you find the protégé threatening, chances are it's not the right protégé for you. If, on the other hand, you sense that,

for some reason, the person finds you threatening to a point where he or she cannot think clearly or talk confidently, or if some other form of obvious intimidation manifests itself, you may want to consider a different protégé. The person you are looking for is a person who admires you, and respects you, but is not overly intimidated by you.

9. **Someone Who Needs What You Can Offer**
   Sometimes the protégé chosen by a mentor is a person who will not make it if someone doesn't care about her. Many mentors are actually much more attracted to the person who needs the special attention they can give her.

Your protégé may not have all these qualities. That's ok. When you find the protégé that is right for you, you will discover that *mentoring* produces a "beautiful compensation" in life. It's a great way to live your dream.

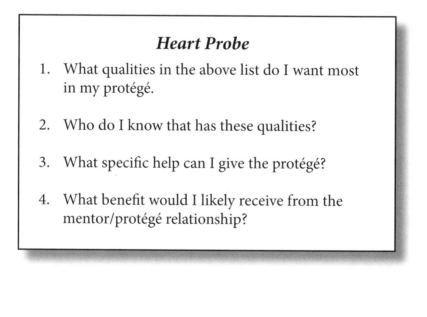

### *Heart Probe*

1. What qualities in the above list do I want most in my protégé.

2. Who do I know that has these qualities?

3. What specific help can I give the protégé?

4. What benefit would I likely receive from the mentor/protégé relationship?

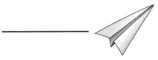

# STEP 4 → Teach Your Team to Dream

*Alone we can do so little;*
*together we can do so much.*
*—Helen Keller*

Teaching others to dream is one of the most rewarding aspects of dreaming big. Your leadership directly influences the quality and direction of other people's lives. And together you accomplish so much more.

Teamwork makes dreaming big work.

Discovering > Refining > Living > **TEACHING** > Encouraging

# Day 22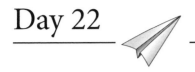

# Demonstrating
# **Leadership**

*Leadership is much more an art, a belief,*
*a condition of the heart, than a set of things to do.*[1]
—*Max De Pree*

## Overview

- *Dreaming*
- *Believing*
- *Serving*

### What kind of leader do you want to be?

Suppose you asked your friends, "What qualities produce a really great leader?" What do you think they would say? Extensive business experience? Natural Skill? An MBA? Max De Pree, former CEO of Herman Miller, asserts that there is an *art* to leadership and that art is affected by your beliefs and the condition of your heart.

In this chapter, we focus on three conditions of the heart we believe are essential to teaching your team to become effective leaders. Although some people seem to acquire these traits automatically because of their natural temperaments, the good news is that anyone can choose to develop these qualities.

As your team members (spouse, family, friends, business associates) see these qualities in you, their confidence in your leadership will increase. They will want to demonstrate the same qualities in relationships they influence.

> *Leaders are made, not born.*
> —PETER DRUCKER

## Dreaming

Great leaders are dreamers. They have the ability to think beyond the immediate. It's a vision of the future. A crystal clear dream is the reason for *leadership*. Leadership is knowing *what* to do next, knowing *why* that is important, and knowing *how* to bring the appropriate resources to bear on the need at hand. Dreaming big is at the heart of what leaders do.

When you teach your team to develop clear dreams, you help them become leaders. They will know how to ask and answer these questions:
- "What do we do next?"
- "Why is this important?"
- "Where can I locate the appropriate resources?"

## Believing

Leaders commit to core beliefs. Beliefs represent the condition of one's heart. Our best leaders have a condition of the heart others want to model.

In broad outline, a leader's effectiveness in teaching others is highly affected by three huge belief systems and the questions they imply:
- **God**
  - o Who is God to me?
  - o What purpose, if any, does He have for my life?
  - o If God has a purpose for my life, how will I know it?

- **Man**
  - o Is man created in the image of God or a product of mere chance?
  - o How does my answer to this question affect my business decisions?
  - o How does my view of man affect my leadership of my team?
- **Life**
  - o How does my belief about God affect my mission in life?
  - o How does my mission in life affect the way I live?
  - o How is my way of life reflective of my Life Dream?

Take time to think through these questions. Notice how beliefs dramatically affected the leadership style of Dr. Martin Luther King, Jr. He believed that God created us with equal worth and dignity. For that reason he dedicated his life to justice for every man. His belief fueled his big dream.

*Let us not wallow in the valley of despair . . . I have a dream that one day this nation will rise up and live out the true meaning of its creed. "We hold these truths to be self-evident that all men are created equal . . . "*

*I have a dream that one day out in the red hills of Georgia the sons of former slaves and the sons of former slave owners will be able to sit down together at the table of brotherhood.*

*I have a dream that one day even the state of Mississippi, a state sweltering with the heat of oppression, will be transformed into an oasis of freedom and justice.*

*I have a dream that my four little children will one day live in a nation where they will not be judged by the color of their skin but by their character.*

*I have a dream today. I have a dream that one day down in Alabama, with its vicious racists, with its governor having his lips dripping with the words of interposition and nullification; that one day right down in Alabama, little black boys and black girls will be able to join hands with little white boys and white girls as if sisters and brothers.*

*I have a dream today. I have a dream that one day every valley shall be engulfed, every hill shall be exalted and every mountain shall be made low, the rough places will be made plains and the crooked places will be made straight and the glory of the Lord shall be revealed and all flesh shall see it together.*[2]

Dr. King is an example of a leader whose dream mobilized millions because of what he believed and demonstrated. Leaders do not apologize for the truth. The beliefs they commit to generate courage in their hearts. Bullies cannot intimidate them.

## Serving

Beliefs affect one's willingness to serve. If you believe you are at the center of your world, you will not serve. If you believe your team exists to serve you, you will not be effective. If you believe that leadership is exercised through power and attempt to control, intimidate, or manipulate your team to do your will, you won't lead long. Your team eventually will work against you.

Human nature does not easily serve others. Jesus said to his team of twelve men, "The one who rules [should be] like the one who serves"[3] He taught them by his own example. "I am among you as one who serves."[4]

Viktor Frankl, an Austrian psychologist, made a significant discovery during his imprisonment in the death camps of Nazi Germany. He watched others who shared in the ordeal and was intrigued with the question of what made it possible for some people to survive when most died. He looked at several factors—health, vitality, family structure, intelligence, survival skills. Finally, he concluded that none of these factors was primarily responsible. He realized the survivors' single, most significant, common characteristic was their belief that they still had a purpose—a compelling conviction of a mission to perform, some important work left to do in serving others.[5]

Effective leadership is based, at least in part, on conditioning your heart for *dreaming, believing,* and *serving,* As a leader, you

> *Everybody can be great . . .*
> *because anybody can serve. You*
> *don't have to have a college degree*
> *to serve.*
> *You don't have to make your*
> *subject and verb agree to serve.*
> *You only need a heart full of*
> *grace. A soul generated by love.*
> —MARTIN LUTHER KING, JR.

know your purpose. You inspire others to follow your lead because, frankly, you are outstanding. Relatively few people know what to do, why it is important, and how to resource it. Most are looking for someone who has this figured out; someone who can paint them a picture of a dream that arises out of deeply held beliefs and who will serve them by teaching them to paint their dreams as well. That's the art of leadership.

### Heart Probe

1. Who do I know that I would describe as an effective leader? To what extent does this person demonstrate the qualities of *dreaming, believing, serving?*

2. What would make me a more effective leader?

# Day 23

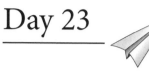

# Recruiting
## a Dream Team

*Today, as never before in history,*
*organizational leaders are realizing*
*that to maximize performance*
*people need to be organized in teams.*[1]
—*Ken Blanchard*

## Overview

- *Identify the Direction of Your Prospect's Dreams*
- *Connect Prospects with Their Motivation*
- *Look for Strong Team Members Who Will Help Others*

**If your Life Dream is so big that you need an organization of like-minded individuals to pursue it, you need to know how to recruit a dream team.**

Not everyone is a team player. How many gifted athletes have you seen blow their careers simply because they refused to use their talent for the good of the team? Teams with exceptionally-talented players who all want to "star" will lose to teams with average ability players who are organized into a team that maximizes everyone's performance.

Coach John Wooden was against the practice of retiring the jersey number of star players on his basketball teams. "The jersey and the number on it never belong to just one player, no matter how great or how big a 'star' that particular player is. It goes against the whole concept of what a team is. The team is the star, never an individual player."[2]

To build a star team, develop the following recruiting skills that will help you integrate the dream energy of each individual into an even bigger dream shared by the entire team.

## Identify the Direction of Your Prospect's Dreams

The first recruiting skill is to find prospects whose dreams match the *direction* of your team dream. The following diagram can help you get a feel for the importance of this concept.

In the diagram, the large arrow is where you're headed—individually and as an organization. It's the team dream. When a person you're interviewing shares her dreams and you find she's headed in the direction of arrow number 1, you know that everything you teach your team will not be what that individual wants to do.

Or suppose you interview a person headed in the direction of arrow number 2.

> *The successful attainment of a dream is a cart and horse affair. Without a team of horses; a cart of dreams can go nowhere.*
> —REX MURPHY

He may say, in essence, "Well, our dreams are at right angles. My dream is not against what you're doing; it's just in a different direction." This person may be with you for a month or a year— however long it takes him to find an opportunity that's going in the direction he wants to go. But in a short period of time he will not be with you because he is not convinced that the way to reach his dream is to go the direction of the team dream. Every day he's going to have to *force* himself to think about your direction because all of his instincts are to head in a different direction.

If a person is going in the direction of arrow number 3, that person might stay with you a lot longer. Her dream is similar to yours, goes in a similar direction, and you could work together for a month to a year or longer. You'll both be moving in the general direction you want to go, but because there is not true alignment, she will eventually leave you.

By now you realize that the people heading in the direction of arrow number 4 are the ones you're really looking for. When you ask these people to describe their dream and whether they think you can help them reach it, the light goes on. They begin to see their dreams becoming a reality with the help of your team. They're excited, energized. Maybe they can't sleep at night. They want to go in the same direction that you are headed. They will be teachable. These are the people you want on your team. Coach Pat Riley notes, "Teamwork requires that everyone's efforts flow in a single direction."[3]

Psychologist Warren Bennis spent years studying 150 corporate leaders. He found that the indispensable first quality of successful leaders is a guiding vision, a clear idea of what they want to do. Bennis says, "All the leaders I know have a strongly defined sense of purpose. And when you have an organization where the people are aligned behind a clearly defined vision or purpose, you get a powerful organization."[4]

## Connect Prospects with Their Motivation

A second recruiting skill is to find prospects who show an overlap of three priorities: a dream they are passionate about; a psychological disposition to do the work to fulfill that dream; and the financial means to make a living in the process. When these three priority circles overlap each other, you have a winning prospect with a powerful motivational force.

Another way of illustrating the idea of finding the right prospect for the right opportunity came from Dr. Ted Engstrom, now deceased. Ted was the president of three major nonprofit organizations and is known worldwide for his management expertise. While we were writing the book, *Boardroom Confidence,*[5] I asked Ted, "What is the bottom line on building a strong team?" I expected a fairly long, complicated, maybe even a hard-to-understand answer. Ted's profoundly simple response was, *"Getting round pegs in round holes."* The longer I look at this bit of wisdom, the more profound it becomes. What you're really trying to do is make sure that each person is inclined to do what he knows will help him achieve his dreams.

Does this mean the dreams of your team members have to be identical? Of course not. But they *do* need to flow in the same direction. The question is not, "Can the candidate do the work?" Einstein could have driven a cab in New York City. The question is: "What does the candidate *want* to do, and can he or she do it effectively in the pursuit of the team dream?"

If you are a leader and you already have a team in place, you could help your team members by teaching them the qualities of a dream team. They will achieve maximum performance when they have the following:

- A crystal clear Life Dream
- An internal drive to pursue that dream
- A willingness to learn and change in order to grow stronger
- A commitment to be a team player.

In other words, find out if you have *round pegs in round holes.* Their dream and your teaching will provide the motivation and energy they need.

## Look for Strong Team Members Who Will Help Others

A third recruiting skill is to find prospects who want to help others. Ron Hale is an example of one who helps others achieve their dreams. Although he makes a great deal of money in his business, he is always serving those less experienced.

One of the favorite experiences of my life, which I think about when I sit in rocking chairs on quiet evenings, was an evening spent with Ron Hale. Ron and I were invited by entrepreneur Angelo D'Amico to speak at a weekend training conference. After our session, which ended around midnight, Angelo invited twenty to thirty of his more promising protégés to come to his suite and have some personal time with Ron Hale. He invited me to sit in.

This spontaneous meeting lasted from midnight until about 4:00 in the morning. Ron Hale, who at the time was in his 60s, could have chosen to be sleeping. But he sat tirelessly and shared the best of his wisdom about how to recruit people, how to spot winners, how to develop a team. He simply shared from his heart the very best of his thinking about how to win in life.

That night I asked myself, why does a man who makes millions go out of his way to speak at a conference, and then stay up from midnight till 4:00 in the morning teaching young leaders how to follow his trail marks in life? My conclusion was that Ron's big dream is not money.

A person cannot be motivated by something they have plenty of. If you've got plenty of food, another sandwich is not motivating to you. If you've got plenty of water, more water is not motivating to you. If you've got plenty of money, more money isn't motivating to you.

Ron Hale is motivated by giving young leaders the opportunity to grow. His big Life Dream provides energy not only late into the night, but for the rest of his life.

We challenge you to recruit people whose dreams are way beyond money, because there will come a day when money will not motivate. Even when income objectives are accomplished, you want people on your team who will keep going, keep building, keep learning, keep growing, keep stretching, and keep helping for as long as there are people to help and needs to be met.

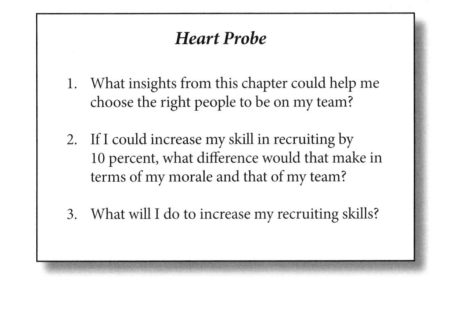

### Heart Probe

1. What insights from this chapter could help me choose the right people to be on my team?

2. If I could increase my skill in recruiting by 10 percent, what difference would that make in terms of my morale and that of my team?

3. What will I do to increase my recruiting skills?

# Asking
# **Dream-Sparking**
# Questions

*A major stimulant to creative thinking is focused questions.*
*There is something about a well-worded question that often penetrates*
*to the heart of the matter and triggers new ideas and insights.*
*—Brian Tracy*

## Overview

- *Ten Diagnostic "Heart Reading" Questions*
- *Assessing Individual Dream Strength*
- *A Dream-Sparking Retreat*

**Asking the right questions helps your team discover their dreams.**

As we mentioned in the last chapter, the question in recruiting a great team is not "Can this person do the work?" But rather, "What does this person actually *want* to do?" Men and women ultimately do what they really want to do far more consistently than what they really do not want to do, but are paid to do.

Until you know the true dreams in the hearts of your prospects, it is unwise if not dangerous to have them on your team. You are only guessing at what really motivates them to contribute to the fullest extent possible.

But, how do you look into a person's heart? How can you see who she is and how motivated she will remain over the next few years? Let me tell you how I came to my top three questions to ask a person that gives me a peek inside his or her heart.

Tom, one of the students at our three-day Advanced Leadership Retreat, asked me a question I'll never forget. "Bobb, if you could only ask only three questions to get to know a person, what three questions would you ask?" My first thought was, "What a great question!" The three I would probably ask are:

1. What is your big dream, your Life Dream?
2. What three major roadblocks are keeping you from your dream?
3. If you could do only three measurable things in the next ninety days to make a 50 percent difference in reaching your dream a year from now, what three things would you do?

## Ten Diagnostic "Heart Reading" Questions

As a result of Tom's question, I decided to expand the concept to ten questions related to teaching a team how to discover their Life Dreams. These questions can help you read what's in a person's heart.

1. What are your dreams?
2. Of all of your dreams, which one is the most important to you long term?
3. Why is this dream so important to you?
4. How confident are you that this is a dream you can actually see become real?
5. If you could do only three measurable things before you die . . . what three things would you do?

6. What dreams have you had in the past that you were able to achieve?

7. What do you see as your single greatest strength? What do you do the very best?

8. What is your "passion" today? What makes you weep with compassion or pound the table in anger?

9. Realistically, what are your three greatest roadblocks today as you think about pursuing your dream?

10. If you could do only three measurable things in the next ninety days to move you toward your dream, what three things would you do?

As you try to get behind the person's small talk or defenses, these questions will help expose what's really going on in the person's heart if he or she cares enough to be candid with you.

## Assessing Individual Dream Strength

The person with a dull, depressing future may be very open to being recruited by you. The person who has an okay, up and down kind of motivation may also be very recruitable. And the person who currently holds an exciting, energizing, motivating position may seem to be the least recruitable—but *that may be the person you want to go after for your team.*

Here is a chart to keep in mind whenever you are interviewing prospective team members to assess the strength of their dreams. The Dream Strength chart gives you an idea of how to categorize their dreams, confidence levels, opportunities, and attitude toward the future.

> *You are never too old to set another goal or to dream a new dream.*
> —C.S. LEWIS

| DREAM STRENGTH | | | |
|---|---|---|---|
| **DREAM** | **CONFIDENCE** | **OPPORTUNITY** | **FUTURE** |
| • No dream<br>• Fuzzy dream<br>• Unrealistic dream | • Low | • None | • Dull<br>• Depressing<br>• Discouraged |
| • Few dreams<br>• Low level dreams<br>• Unrealistic dreams | • Medium | • Some — not great | • OK<br>• Average<br>• Up and down emotionally |
| • Clear dreams<br>• Major dreams<br>• Realistic dreams | • High | • Great | • Exciting<br>• Energizing<br>• Motivating |

## A Dream-Sparking Retreat

As you coach your team members individually or at team meetings, you will constantly be asking them dream-sparking questions. But consider taking your team away for a one-day dream-sparking retreat. The benefit of a retreat is that normally there is more time to focus, to reflect, to understand, and to implement.

You may use the following ideas to adapt the dream-sparking questions in Dreaming Big to your team setting:

1.  Pick your ten favorite dream-sparking questions from any section of Dreaming Big or from your past experience.

2.  Adapt the wording of the questions if necessary to fit your team's goals.

3.  Put the questions on one or two pages with space between each question for your team to jot down their thoughts.

4.  Give the questions to team members before the retreat so they can reflect on their answers before being asked to express their opinions at the retreat.

Although the questions will go deep into what matters to your team, this is not a time to be overly introspective. Your team members will be most willing to probe their hearts and share their thoughts if the atmosphere is open, supportive, and each team member follows your example of communicating honestly and listening deeply. It's a great way to celebrate the unique dreams of your team.

---

### *Heart Probe*

1.  What difference could it make if I were to ask my team members the ten diagnostic "heart reading" questions?

2.  How would assessing the dream strength of my team members assist me in teaching them to dream?

3.  If I were to plan a Dream-Sparking Retreat, where could I have it? How do I think a retreat setting would help my team to dream big?

---

# Day 25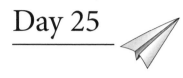

# Building a Team on
# Core Values

*It is essential that we have a culture of values-based leaders
with integrity and passion to set a vision, to inspire
their organizations to align around that vision, and to nurture
greatness in those around them.*
*—William C. Weldon*

## Overview

- *Building on a Secure Foundation*
- *Teaching Core Values to Your Team*
- *Molding Individuals into High Performance Teams*

**Is your team aware of the core values that fuel your Life Dream?**

People make decisions based on what they passionately value.
The dream of Martin Luther King, Jr. energized countless people
in many nations, states, counties, and cities because it was built on
values recognized worldwide as core.

*A core value is a principle, standard, or quality regarded
as essential.* It forms the center of what is most important to
organizations as well as individuals. Teams without agreement on
core values have lifeless, plodding, bureaucratic organizations. High

performance teams are committed not only to a shared dream but to a shared set of values.

## Building on a Secure Foundation

How do we build a foundation strong enough to withstand the winds of adversity, the rains of frustration, the storms of fierce competition? We believe the process is simple and extremely significant:

- Identify core values you see as essential for your business
- Build concensus with key team members regarding the values you share
- Develop your organizational focus on these shared values.

If you go to the website of major corporations, you'll find that many of them list their core values. For example, Office Depot lists five key values: *Integrity; Innovation; Inclusion; Customer Focus; Accountability.* ServiceMaster believes service based on their values is a key to their success. Why? Values provide a conceptual guideline for consistent decisions. They promote corporate identity and marketing brand. Foundational values clarify the culture you want your team to demonstrate.

## Teaching Core Values to Your Team

You may find four fundamental steps helpful in teaching your team members to build their dream on a foundation of core values.

1. **First identify the top five core values at the center of your team dream.**
   If there were only five values that you felt were the very core of what you believe about your dream—the critical nature of it, the internal essence of it, what you wanted the whole team never to loose track of, the non-negotiables—what would those five core values for your dream be? Be very explicit, very clear, very precise. Make a list, and once the list is completed, talk with your team or a friend about your

top five. See if they agree with you that a particular value is a core value. You may also want to rank them: which is number one, which is number two, etc.

Paul's wife, Janiece, is a business owner in the process of building a strong business team. At first she thought she could not come up with five core values that fuel her dream and could be shared by the team. But she got started and then became enthusiastic about the process. Her list of business values may stimulate your own thinking.

1.   Dream Building
2.   Hope Giving
3.   Integrity
4.   Teachability
5.   Profitability

2.   **Once you have defined your top five core values, practice teaching them with passion.**
     Practice talking on the video about your core values with all the passion you can muster. Express how you feel deeply about those five values. Imagine that one of your team members says, "That number three there, that isn't important at all." Respond, with your reasons why you are deeply committed to this core value. Then review the video as if you were the skeptic or a new team member. Would you be convinced? If not, keep thinking, keep practicing, keep sharing your thoughts about what matters most to you *until it's second nature to you and you can actually feel the deep emotion.*

3.   **Teach your team the core values of your dream.**
     Sometimes a team member is recruited who does not have a clear or holistic understanding of the breadth and depth of the values important to you. Once he learns what your values are, he may realize that he doesn't share those values. He may choose to leave your team. That's OK. It's essential that you and your team are in 100 percent agreement as to the core values on which you want to build your organization.

As Laurie Beth Jones says in her book, *Teach Your Team to Fish*, the role of a team is to *"pull together as a team without pulling each other apart."*[1] If team members do not agree on the core values, it likely will lead to in-fighting, misunderstanding, splits, and power struggles.

Sometimes team members lose resolve or momentum because they misjudge the motives of the team leader. You *can only teach what you model.* If you *live* your top five values, reviewing them with your team can affirm your integrity and establish a strong bond between you and your team members. If your values inspire you, there is a good chance they will inspire your team.

4. **The key to transferring core values into team activity is process. Process is simply flow-charting.**
   What are the five to ten most fundamental processes in your organization? What are the things you do over and over and over again that you need to teach? For some organizations it's prospecting, contacting, teaching, selling, closing, servicing. What is the *process* new team members need to know and follow to be successful?

   Your team members need to see a clear connection between the *values* they believe in and the *activities* they need to do to be successful. For example, you could say to your team, "Here is the process we have found most effective in order for you to achieve the growth you value."

## Molding Individuals Into High Performance Teams

When your team unites around a big dream built on values that inspire them, that challenge them to greatness, that motivate them to tackle problems with confidence, you will have a high performance team that succeeds.

As you sense our excitement about the power of dreaming big, you may think we're saying you can take a team of people without talent, without ability, without experience, without anything going for them, and in a matter of weeks put together a championship team—just because you've got a big dream. Wrong!

Building high performance teams, whether in athletics or business or ministry, typically takes years. In athletics, for example, it's very rare when an expansion team makes the playoffs in the first year, let alone the championship. Even with a clear dream, it generally takes years of discipline, hard work, subtle adjustments, and great coaching to mold a team into a world-class unit—to help a group of *individuals* in the same uniform really become a *team* with the same dream. One of the best ways to move your team from wherever it is to its highest performance is to teach and duplicate your team's core values.

## *Heart Probe*

1. Review core values in other organizations. Are there some values I need to adopt to better represent who I am?

2. Think about a team on which I have played (or team I have watched) that truly functioned as a team. What made the team successful?

3. As I review my core values, how do I plan to teach them to my team?

# Day 26

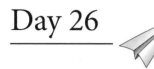

# Helping Your
## Team See the
# **Big Picture**

*Two men look out through the same bars:*
*One sees the mud, and one the stars.*[1]
*—American Proverb*

### Overview

- *Time: Dreaming Long Term*
- *Width: Dreaming Globally*
- *Depth: Dreaming Transformationally*

### What is your dominant outlook on life?

The brutal fact about the way many go through life is that they see only the dust and dirt—heads down, hearts heavy, and spirits low. They feel imprisoned by past mistakes as well as present routines. Overwhelmed by a sense of futility, they are caught in a mental rut and don't know how to break free.

It may be there are people on your team who are in that situation. You may feel "imprisoned" at times yourself. Frankly, most do. We all must deal with work situations that frustrate, budgets that constrain, relationships that appear to be hopeless. In the midst of it all, the key question is "What is our outlook?" Will we see the mud or the stars?

*Big Picture* refers to intentionally looking for and seeing the shinning stars. Outside the rut of everyday schedules, there's a big beautiful world waiting to benefit from what you and your team can contribute. To help your team members see the big picture, teach them how to take a three-dimensional look at their dreams:

- the length of *time* it will take for them to be fulfilled;
- the breadth of *space* their dreams will cover; and
- the depth of *impact* their dreams will make in people's lives.

## Time: Dreaming Long Term

Without a big picture perspective on the length of time you have to fulfill your dreams, you will feel pressured, discouraged, overwhelmed . . . like the bulldozer is about to push you over the edge of the mountain. You get the awful feeling of living from day-to-day, from hand-to-mouth, from emergency-to-emergency, from season-to-season.

Free yourself with the practical truth that

- Big dreams take time . . . often decades, and
- Patience is a virtue . . . for your team and yourself.

The bigger your dream is, the bigger your time perspective needs to be. Keep yourself and your team thinking practically about the time dimension. Encourage yourself and your team to dream long term.

### One Year

Frequently one of the things that causes time pressure is that you don't have a track record. You and your team have never done what you're planning to do. Therefore, you tend to set unrealistically high standards.

If you're taking on a new venture, set very realistic standards and meet them. If you don't meet them at first, analyze the causes, reset the time frame, and recommit to the priority. Keep doing this until you succeed. Then you will be encouraged by your success. You'll be able to expand your priorities for getting things done during the second year. Typically, if you give yourself a two-year time frame to accomplish what you hope to achieve in one year, you'll find it turns out to be more *realistic*.

## Four Years

The first day you take on a new venture in the pursuit of your dream, you begin a journey that has a time frame. Before it gets to the point where you feel it's "going your way," it likely will take four years. It may take that long before you see evidence that your venture is "off the ground."

The first year tends to be a year of orientation. You're getting the feel of what the key variables are, who the people are, and what the roadblocks are.

The second year is experimental. You're beginning to try things that you think will probably be the solution. You are prototyping what you think will work, revising it, and deciding whether or not the revision works. Caution: at some point early in your pursuit, you may get the feeling, "It will never work."

The third year is evaluation. Some things worked better than you had planned or dreamed, some about the same, and some you decide to stop altogether based on actual experience.

But at about four years, you will get a fair assessment of how successful you will be. *You know what you know and you are ready to go!* Why this rule of thumb works, I don't know. But I've talked to many major developers and they all agree . . . it takes about four years.

## Five Years

Progress is typically a function of time, energy, and money. The more money you have, the less time it will take, and the less energy, or people, or staff it will take. If you're limited on your money and people, it's going to take a lot of time.

Keep in mind that most progress is not strictly linear. Results in any area don't start and go up and up and up in a straight line. They tend to be slow in the first year or two or three, and then grow faster and faster in the later years. At the end of five years, you likely will find that much more progress has been made than you would have imagined when you started.

## Ten Years

Teach your team to pursue their dreams so that ten years from today, they will be at their peak. Ask them to imagine themselves looking the best, feeling the best, being more effective than they've ever been. But every year on their birthday, stretch it out one year, so that when they're 40, they're just getting ready to be 50 . . . and when they're 50, they're just getting ready to be 60, and so on.

The ten-year time frame positions your team to be *lifelong students*. Then they never get to the point where they think, "I've arrived. I don't need to contribute to the team anymore." They will have a future orientation rather than feeling as if their peak is in the past.

## Eternity

There will come a time for each of us when God will step into our personal history and decree that time shall be no more. It seems to me that one of the reasons God gives us prayer is to force us to an eternal perspective in time. The minute my knee touches the carpet, the reality strikes me that I am entering a dimension of reality bigger than time. Someday the pressures I feel or the deadlines I face will not even exist.

Paul and I find it immensely helpful to see our time pressures on earth in light of eternity. One of Paul's professors taught him a motto for life he has never forgotten: *sub specie infinitas—Live your life under the viewpoint of eternity.* We believe that every injustice or act of

> *A man tends to over-estimate what he can do in one year . . . And under-estimate what he can do in five.*
> —Ted Engstrom

cruelty suffered by believers here on earth will be more than compensated during the first "minutes" in the splendor of heaven.

If you or your team members feel imprisoned by time, ask these questions:

- What can I stop, postpone, or delay to better pursue my Life Dream?
- Can adding money or people reduce the length of time required?
- When I see the bigger time picture, what new insights can I pass on to my team?

## Width: Dreaming Globally

The second dimension in your 3D perspective is to consider how broad your dream is. Will your Life Dream concern only you? Will it touch lives in your city, your nation, your world?

Mike Downey founded Global Missions Fellowship. Whenever you see Mike, he is optimistic, encouraged, focused, and excited about the future. He built a great team of people, a budget of millions of dollars a year, and GMF has involved thousands of people internationally.

When asked, "How do you keep your dream so clearly fixed in your mind?" he said, "I spend a day a month away by myself, looking at the dream, planning next steps toward the dream, keeping the coals alive, fanning the fire, doing anything I can to make the dream more real in my mind and my heart." What would happen if you took your team away periodically to broaden their focus for the future?

> **DREAMING BIG**
> *Our goal isn't just to achieve the American dream. We also want to share it with others—around the U.S., in India, or wherever the journey takes us*
> —CHETAN & VINEETA RASTOGI

# Depth: Dreaming Transformationally

The third dimension of a big picture perspective is the depth of your team's dreams in terms of personal relationships. What impact will their individual dreams and your shared dreams have on other people?

Did you know that in America today:

- Three out of five mothers with children under age six feel the need to work outside the home to survive financially

> *We make a living by what we get, But we make a life by what we give.*
>
> —WINSTON CHURCHILL

- Two-thirds of school age children live with a single employed parent
- 1 in 20 adults is not literate in English.

Worldwide, the need for help is staggering:

- Six million children, and even more adults, die unnecessarily every day
- 5,500 babies died from preventable respiratory infections today
- One billion of the world's children go to bed hungry every night
- In the world today there are about one billion adults who can neither read nor write.

In a *Time* magazine cover story entitled "How to Save a Life," Bono writes,

> *The numbers are so big that they can numb us into indifference: 5,000 people dying every day from tuberculosis, 1 million dying every year from malaria. Behind each of these statistics is someone's daughter, someone's son, a mother, a father, a sister, a brother. We cannot save every life. But the ones we can, we must.* [2]

How many of these problems could be reversed? What could your team do if you teach them to dream dreams that transform lives? What price tag could you put on even one life saved?

Let us think about the depth of the dreams by which we inspire our teams. If our concern for our children and their children and the children of the world lacks commitment and passion, then we bow to the difficulty; we stay as we are and drift. But if, as Norman Cousins writes, "we have some feeling for the gift of life and the uniqueness of life, if we have confidence in freedom, growth, and the miracle of vital change, then difficulty loses its power to intimidate."[3]

In a speech entitled, "Where We're Going," businesswoman Pam Winters inspired thousands of business owners with her passionate vision of what the future can hold when their dreams include the transformation of lives.

*We're not done yet. We've got a long way to go. We're just getting started. We see this thing really big. We see . . . thousands and thousands and thousands of lives being changed for the good; moms coming home to raise their own children, if that's what they want to do; marriages getting stronger; this country being changed—one person at a time. We are so proud of our team.*[4]

What picture do you see? What picture does your team see?

## Heart Probe

1.  How would I describe the three dimensions of
    my dream?
    >    What is the length of time?
    >    What is the breadth of influence?
    >    What is the depth of personal impact?

2.  What practical difference will it make for my
    team to grasp the Big Picture dimensions of our
    dreams?

# Day 27

## **Equipping**
## Your Team to
## **Overcome Failure**

*Failures are finger posts on the road to achievement.*
*—C.S. Lewis*

### Overview

- *Expect Your Success to be Built on Failure*
- *Learn from Failure*
- *Develop a Framework for Managing Failure*
- *Become Mentally Tough*

**Failures never signal the end—unless you quit.**

Failures are finger posts pointing us forward in our journey. They help us realize we have not yet arrived. They tell us our dream destination is still down the road. They say, "Get up! This way! Keep going!"

What if you were able to teach this attitude about failure to your team? What difference would it make when people throw roadblocks in their way, when hoped for outcomes do not materialize, when a tragedy strikes? Would it make them stronger entrepreneurs?

*Entrepreneur* is derived from an old French word meaning "the undertaker." The word came to mean a person who undertakes the risk of a business venture. Most businessmen and women face decisions everyday that carry risk of failure. If we are not well prepared mentally—if our minds are soft, our thinking undisciplined, our reasoning muscle out of shape—we jeopardize not only our business, but also our health. If entrepreneurs don't train for testing times, they very well could face an early call from . . . the other "undertaker."

This chapter provides four principles that help you coach your team to face risks, to overcome setbacks, and to develop a strength mentality.

> *A diamond cannot be polished without friction, nor a man perfected without trials.*
> —CHINESE PROVERB

## Expect Your Success to be Built on Failure

John Crowe, a very successful businessman, was attacked, shot, robbed, and left for dead. Through an amazing sequence of events, the love and prayers of his family and thousands of friends, and by the grace of God, his life was spared. He could have given up fighting for life. He could have let fear overwhelm him, preventing him from achieving his goals. But he knew firsthand that, as he says, *"success is based on failure."*[1]

Think of very successful people who failed.

- Abraham Lincoln entered the Black Hawk War as a captain and came out as a private.
- Thomas Edison's boyhood teacher told him he was too stupid to learn anything.
- Leo Tolstoy, author of *War and Peace*, flunked out of college.
- Babe Ruth spent his childhood years in an orphanage

and, as a baseball player, struck out 1,330 times—on his way to the Hall of Fame.

- Elvis Presley was banished from the Grand Ole Opry after one performance and was told: "You ain't goin' nowhere, son."
- Michael Jordan was cut from his high school basketball team.
- Oprah Winfrey was fired from her television reporter's job and advised: "You're not fit for TV."

What kept these famous failures going? If you check their biographies, you will find a common theme: *they refused to quit.* They regrouped, modified their approach, developed further skill, and with fresh knowledge and experience, tried again. They learned from their failures.

We may be slow to learn from failures for several reasons. We are surprised by failure. We don't expect to fail. We see failure as an enemy, not a teacher. We are horrified at the prospect of failing, so when it naturally occurs we become defensive, depressed, immobilized, or even pretend it has not occurred. We are not prepared to learn from it.

Obviously it's not enough simply to expect to fail. Improvement must be expected as well. Usually we need a minor adjustment, a little more time, and lots more patience. Perhaps our knowledge of the product or the relationship we have with the client has not yet reached the level of providing competitive advantage. When we expect tough times to come and customers to raise objections and logistical nightmares to happen, we are better prepared to build success on our failures.

## Learn from Failure

You've probably known that sickening feeling: you think everyone in the world must know you've failed, and you have to force yourself just to keep your head up.

What has been the biggest failure in your life? Maybe it was seeing the pink slip when your company downsized. Maybe it was losing a huge account or not closing the biggest sale of your career. Maybe you said or did something that caused people to lose their confidence in you or your business.

Whatever it was, have you responded to the finger posts raised by your failure? Have you resolved any lingering negative emotions? Do you know how to help your team accurately assess and learn from their failures? Asking the following questions gives a framework for learning to solve problems.

> *A smooth sea never made a skillful mariner.*
> —ENGLISH PROVERB

1.  **Did I fail because of another person, because of my situation, or because of myself?**
    If you conclude the fault really was your own, say to yourself, "All right, what did I learn? And what else do I need to learn to keep me from failing like that in the future? Is there someone I need to reconcile with?"

2.  **Did I actually fail, or did I simply fall short of an unrealistically high standard?**
    If you don't reach all your goals, you can regroup, adjust the goal, and restart. Decide the changes you need to make in order to be more realistic in the standard you set for yourself.

    > *There is no doubt in my mind that there are many ways to be a winner, but there is only one way to be a loser and that is to fail and not look beyond the failure.*
    > —KYLE ROTE, Jr.

3.  **Where did I succeed as well as fail?**
    As you reflect on your failure, make a list of all the ways in

which you feel you succeeded or did what was right in that situation.

4. **What lessons have I learned?**
   What personal wisdom and resolve can you learn from your failures?

5. **Do I feel absolved from guilt over the failure?**
   If your failure was a moral failure of some kind, have you asked the other person to forgive you? If the guilt is shared to some degree by another, ask the greatest healing question, "Will you forgive me for my contribution to the problem?" If your failure was in any way disobedience of God's law, confess it to Him. Ask your pastor or spiritual leader for help.[2]

   > *Failure is the tuition you pay for success.*
   >
   > —WALTER BRUNELL

6. **How can I turn the failure into success?**
   Can yesterday's failure be part of your success tomorrow? Can you turn the "lemon" into lemonade? What have you learned that you can pass on to others?

7. **Practically speaking, where do I go from here?**
   What are your plans? By when? How?

## Become Mentally Tough

*Do you demonstrate mental toughness?*

Abraham Lincoln showed unwavering toughness even under intense criticism. "I do the very best I know how—the very best I can—and mean to keep doing so until the end. If the end brings me out right, what is said against me won't amount to anything. If the end brings me out wrong, ten angels swearing I was right would make no difference."

Your most effective teaching will be your personal example. Mental strength prevents you from becoming too eager to please others. It keeps you from letting the criticism of others dictate your choices.

*Do you know your stuff?*

Keep in mind that confidence is built on predictability. Predictability is based on deep knowledge of what you do. Deep knowledge is achieved when you know your stuff so well you can answer any objection. It frees you from intimidation. You are able to present your business dream to a skeptic with assured confidence. If you're not there yet, study your material, think it through, and practice until it is *in you.*

It also helps to remember the mentally tough perspective of President Theodore Roosevelt.

> "In the battle of life, it is not the critic who counts; nor the one who points out how the strong person stumbled, or where the doer of a deed could have done better. The credit belongs to the person who is actually in the arena; whose face is marred by dust and sweat and blood, who strives valiantly; who errs and comes short again and again . . . Far better it is to dare mighty things, to win glorious triumphs even though checkered by failure, than to rank with those timid spirits who neither enjoy nor suffer much because they live in the grey twilight that knows neither victory or defeat."

*Do you renew your mind?*

We are constantly bombarded with negative media messages. To keep a strong, positive perspective, we need to have a system for renewing our minds—a daily reading, a quiet time for reflection, a devotional time for prayer and inspiration. Find a system that is true and works for you—one that lifts you up emotionally, that clears the fog mentally, and fires your creative juices.

# *Heart Probe*

1.  What has been my greatest personal failure in the past six months? What lessons can I learn from the failure?

2.  What failure is common to my team? What lessons can we all learn from the failure?

3.  What failure still has a negative hold on me or my team? What actions will increase future success?

4.  What will I do to develop mental toughness personally?

# Day 28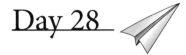

# Creating
# **Competitive**
## Advantage

*Champions aren't made in gyms.*
*Champions are made from something they have*
*deep inside them—a desire, a dream, a vision.*
*—Muhammad Ali*

## Overview

- *Selling Yourself*
- *Selling Your Team*
- *Selling Your Product*
- *Selling Your Advantage*

**If your work includes selling an idea or product, do you know you have the advantage of a champion?**

Do you have a dream that is so strong you are determined to face the blows from your competitors, go the distance, endure the pain, gain the advantage, and win? *If you're not quite there, this chapter is for you.*

Our goal in *Dreaming Big* is to help you to dramatically increase your effectiveness. To do that, you will need to have a strong competitive advantage in four key areas.

## Selling Yourself

Before you can sell your company, your products, and services to anybody, you must first sell them to yourself. In your heart of hearts, how do you answer these questions?

- What is the primary reason I am personally committed to my business?
- Why do I feel my products and services are a superior value?
- What makes me want to buy or use them?
- Did I commit to my company because I believed this company could help me realize my Life Dream?

## Selling Your Team

In recruiting team members, priority questions would be:

- What are your dreams?
- How satisfied are you with your progress toward your dreams?
- Can you see how this organization could serve as a vehicle to help you reach *your* dreams faster?

Notice the focus on the recruit's dreams. The number one motivation for your team members to join you is so *their dreams* can be realized—not yours. The minute you lose track of this fact, you diminish your ability to inspire them to personal achievement and high performance records.

## Selling Your Products

Now assuming *you* started your business or joined your company to turn your dreams into reality, and your *team members* joined your organization to turn their dreams into reality, is it any mystery that your *customers* come to you for help in turning their dreams into reality?

There are five questions for your team to discuss so they can clearly understand why customers buy what they're selling.

1. Who are my customers?
2. What are their needs or dreams?
3. Without my products or services, how would their needs be met?
4. With my products or services, can I meet a need or help them reach their dream?
5. If I were the customer, would I buy the product for the price I'm asking?

Whenever your customers say,

Yes . . . I can imagine myself with the product or service!

Yes . . . I want your product/service.

Yes . . . I see it helping me reach my dreams.

Yes . . . I can pay for it.

Yes . . . this is the right time.

then they will also say, "YES . . . I'LL TAKE IT!"

Use the chart on the following page to determine where your customers may be in their decision process.

# DECISION PROCESS

**IMAGINATION + DESIRE + CONFIDENCE + DREAM + TIMING = A SALE!**
**(If any one step is missing . . . no sale!)**

| | | Imagination | Desire | Confidence | Dream | Timing | Sale! |
|---|---|---|---|---|---|---|---|
| **S A L E S** | **Q U E S T I O N S** | Can the customer imagine using our product or service? | Would they even want to use our product / service if they could? | Is our customer confident they can afford your product or service? | Does our product or service help them get to their needs or dreams faster? | Is this the right time to buy our product or service? | Are they ready to buy? |
| **C U S T O M E R** | **R E S P O N S E S** | No—Can't imagine self with product / service. | Automatic No! | Automatic No! | No, don't want it! | Not applicable | NO! |
| | | Yes—can imagine self with product / service. | No, I don't see us changing suppliers. | No, don't believe I can afford it. | No, not a step toward my needs. | No use to us now. | Probably No. |
| | | Yes | Yes, there may be some reasons for us to consider | Yes, possibly. | Yes, a step toward my dreams. | Not the right time. | Perhaps Yes. |
| | | Yes, I can see myself with the product or service! | Yes, I can picture myself with your product/ service. | Yes, I am confident I can pay for it. | Yes, I see it fitting my dreams perfectly. | Yes, this is the right time! | YES! I'll take it! |

# Selling the Advantage

Whenever you're selling, it's essential to position your competitive advantage in the mind of the buyer, including a dream advantage. Study your own company and your products/services to see exactly how your team can best present your competitive advantages. Also study how your competitors are presenting their goods or services. What do you do better?

Here are the eight key areas to find your competitive advantage.

- Dream advantage
- Convenience advantage
- Emotional advantage
- Loyalty advantage
- Name brand/image advantage
- Price advantage
- Service advantage
- Technical advantage

Using the following chart, discuss with your team what competitive advantages your team is trying to plant in the customer's mind. In the appropriate column, simply rate how you think your company scores in each of the eight advantages: **H**—high, **M**—medium, or **L**—low. In the "100 points" column, imagine that you only have 100 points to spend on all eight advantages. Apportion those 100 points according to the value you think should be placed on each advantage.

Now rank the three highest scoring advantages. Number one should be getting your primary attention. Number two gets the second amount of attention, etc.

## COMPETITIVE ADVANTAGES

| *Eight Advantages* | Examples of Each Advantage | Our Sales & Advertising Focus (Rate each Advantage High, Medium, or Low) | Point Value (Assign points in the eight advantages to total 100) | Our Priority Focus (Rank the three highest scoring advantages 1, 2, & 3) | Competitor's Priority Focus (What appears to be their priorities? Rate: 1, 2, 3) |
|---|---|---|---|---|---|
| **1** **Convenience** advantage *(Tangible)* | • Internet access 24/7 • Delivery options | | | | |
| **2** **Dreams** advantage *(Intangible)* | • Beautiful skin • Youthful appearance • Balanced nutrition | | | | |
| **3** **Emotional** advantage *(Intangible)* | Customer needs we are trying to meet • Love • Significance • Admiration • Recognition • Appreciation • Security • Respect • Acceptance | | | | |
| **4** **Loyalty** advantage *(Tangible)* | • Made in the USA • Personal support | | | | |
| **5** **Name brand / Image** advantage *(Tangible)* | • IBM • Office Depot • Bass Pro • Circuit City | | | | |
| **6** **Price** advantage *(Tangible)* | • Competitive • Lowest cost per use • Special sales | | | | |
| **7** **Services** advantage *(Tangible)* | • Award-winning customer service • Satisfaction guarantee | | | | |
| **8** **Technical** advantage *(Tangible)* | • Product updates • Research & development | | | | |

Dreaming Big

If you study the top ten sales people in any field, you'll find that they have the ability to get inside the customer's mind and heart—not just talk *at* them. The top 10 percent ask the right questions to understand the customer's needs or dreams and to motivate the customer to buy their product or service. The bottom 90 percent are stuck selling technical superiority or convenience or loyalty to a brand name.

In your contacts with customers, keep these three questions clearly in mind:

- What does this person really want?
- Why do they want it?
- How does my product or service help them get what they want?

*Remember, you can sell most anything when you make the connection between your products and your customers' needs or dreams.*

---

### *Heart Probe*

1. To whom have I had trouble selling my products/services? With that person in mind, how would I answer the three questions above?

2. Based on my review of the *Competitive Advantage Chart*, how can our team develop more effective strategies?

---

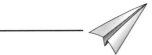

# STEP 5 → Encouraging Your Team

*Two are better than one,*
*because they have a good return for their work.*
*If one falls down, his friend can help him up.*
*—Qoheleth*

When you listen to team members, you cheer them up. You encourage them to win in pursuit of a Life Dream. And when you encourage your team, even though they don't do things exactly right, you will have a good return for your work. You'll have friends for life.

Discovering > Refining > Living > Teaching > **ENCOURAGING**

# Day 29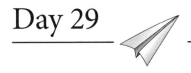

# Listening

*Listen to me for a day . . . an hour . . . a moment—*
*lest I expire in my terrible wilderness, my lonely silence!*
*O God, is there no one to listen?*
> —*Seneca, 4 B.C.*

## Overview

- *Choose to Listen*
- *Create Open Doors*
- *Ask for Clarification*
- *Ask Encouraging Questions*

**Can you name ten people who listen intently to you?**

Do have friends who can think your thoughts before you, empathize with you, and know how to help you clear the doubt and fog you feel? Few of us can. And as Seneca reminds us, this problem is not new.

You likely know a few people who have mastered the skill of listening—a teacher or friend, a brother or sister, a mother or father, a counselor or pastor. When you talk with them, they make you feel you are the only one who matters to them at the moment. Because they listen well, you feel respected as a person. You find yourself quickly getting to the essence of what you want to say. You are motivated to dream big dreams. You are encouraged.

*What would it mean to your team if you listened to them really well?* Research shows that with a few small adjustments, *anyone* can develop the habit of being a better listener. You can.

## Choose to Listen

Three common barriers block the habit of listening well:
- *Stress*—a feeling of pressure from all sides making it difficult to concentrate on the person talking to you.
- *Narcissism*—a natural tendency to focus on your own thoughts and concerns.
- *Brain speed*—although the average speech rate is about 200 words per minute, we can think about four times that speed, tempting the brain to take all kinds of excursions while someone is talking to you.

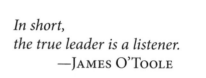

*In short,*
*the true leader is a listener.*
—James O'Toole

Each of these barriers can be overcome by consciously choosing to listen. If you experience some unavoidable distraction, it may be best to solve the problem first. But let your team member know you really want to hear what they are saying. Set a time to get back to focusing your attention on them. When you get back to them in a timely manner, and rarely allow interruptions, you gain credibility as a listener. By modeling this habit for your team, you create an encouraging environment.

## Create Open Doors

When you ask questions and listen actively, your mind is fully engaged. You are better able to concentrate on what is being said and provide understanding feedback. This encourages your team members to continue thinking and to gain clarity. You open the door that promotes communication flow.

Keys that unlock the communication door include the following:

*Tell me about you.*
*What's happening in your life?*
*Tell me more.*
*Then what happened?*
*Let's discuss it.*
*You have something on your mind.*

Door Openers convey a *language of acceptance*; a clear message that the person is important and his or her thoughts matter to you. You create an open door for the flow of communication. You model a listening style that your team will model.

> *When you say, "Tell me about you," you invite people to talk about whatever is most important to them—what they care about, what they dream about, what they hope for, what they fear. It's a brilliant question. It's the key that unlocks another's soul.[1]*
> —Dan DeVos

## Ask for Clarification

In addition to these Door Openers, *feedback* is another technique in listening that is an essential skill in understanding your team. Feedback asks for clarification or repeats in your own words what you heard in order to verify your understanding of the message. You do not add your opinions or evaluations until you are absolutely certain you fully understand—and the one talking to you is satisfied you understand. With surprising consistency, feedback encourages your conversational partners to get to the "heart" of what they think and feel. It corrects our natural tendency to make assumptions—often *wrong* assumptions based on inadequate information.

When you give skillful feedback to your team, you signal that you really are listening to them, not just hearing their words. You convey your desire to understand. You send a powerful teambuilding message of encouragement.

## Ask Encouraging Questions

One of the most neglected people building skills is the ability to ask good questions. Some think asking questions is a sign of weakness or prying into another's business. Others concentrate so hard on what they want to say that asking questions never crosses their minds. But people who do practice the art of asking questions generally report four major benefits:

1. Earning the right to be heard.
2. Meeting a need for attention in other people.
3. Establishing rapport and winning friends.
4. Learning something new.

To make sure you experience these benefits, use the right method of asking questions. Here are a few techniques to draw upon.

*Recognize the emotions involved in every encounter.*
>If a team member is shy, restrain your exuberance. Avoid questions that put the person in the hot seat. Try to mimic their temperament style.

*Make your purpose clear.*
>Noted pollster George Gallup says that when you ask questions, the other person wonders, "Why does he want to know?" When you state your purpose, even if it's "just for information," you break down that barrier. For example, you could say, "In order for me to know best how to help you move forward, what is your sales goal for next month?"

*Begin with questions that are easily answered; then move to open-ended questions that draw out the other person's thoughts and dreams.*
>For example, "Did you like what you heard in our training

session?" can be answered Yes or No. It gives you important, but *minimal* information. Then ask, "What part of the presentation did you like best?" This open ended question will give you more helpful information.

Consider how some of the following questions might encourage your team members not only to dream, but also to actively pursue their dreams.

- Are you doing what you've always wanted to be doing?
- What would you like to be doing?
- In what area of your life would you like to see change this year—and how can I help you?
- What do you feel is holding you back in any aspect of your life—and how can I help you overcome it?
- What is the single area of your life that you would most like me to encourage you in this year?
- What do you consider your three greatest strengths and how can I help you maximize them?
- In what area would you like to see me grow this year? Is this an area that you feel you could help in, or suggest someone who could?
- What is your dream or vision for the long term?
- What would have to happen for you to actively pursue your Life Dream?

In order for these questions to yield honest and meaningful responses, they must be asked without a hint of a judgmental attitude. Your words and demeanor need to convey that you can be trusted and will not misuse the information.

When you listen well, you encourage your team. You create the condition not only for highly functioning teammates, but for lasting friendships as well.

## *Heart Probe*

1. On a scale of 1 to 10, how would I rate myself as a listener? \_\_\_\_

2. On a scale of 1 to 10, how do I think my team members would rate me as a listener? \_\_\_\_

3. If I feel a need to improve my listening skills in order to be a more effective leader, what adjustments do I need to make?
   \_\_\_\_ Choosing to overcome the barriers to listening well
   \_\_\_\_ Creating open doors for conversation to flow
   \_\_\_\_ Asking for clarification
   \_\_\_\_ Asking encouraging questions

# Day 30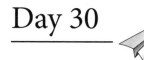

# Building

*Lift people up when they fall.*
*Allow people to be human and make mistakes.*
*If you see someone drop the ball,*
*encourage that guy to get back in the game.* [1]
—Pat Williams

## Overview

- *Building Confidence*
- *Building Hope*
- *Building Relationships*

**How good are you at building up other people?**

*Edify* comes from the same root word as edifice or building. It conveys the image of strength, stability, and reaching for the stars. In this chapter we look at three ways you can edify or cheer your team to get back in the game.

Edifying the members of your team yields unusual pleasure. You notice a deep form of satisfaction comes from building strength into

> *When you edify a person, you literally build them up in the minds of other persons and, perhaps most importantly, in their own mind, too.*[2]
> —Bob Burg

your teammates. When they confidently face opposition and win, you feel you have won.

## Building Confidence

Who is your cheerleader? Who upgrades you, gives you support, cheers you on, especially during the tough moments? Hopefully you have at least one person who does that for you. In any case, intuitively you know how valuable such a person is. You know that one person can spark a whole team to become champions.

Who do you cheer? If you want to be a winning coach for your team, use every encounter as an opportunity to coach, to guide, and to critique with honest, supportive candor. Teach your team to be teachable. Make sure they know you are *for* them. Coach them to listen, make adjustments, and improve. When you help them improve their performance/results, you build confidence like nothing else.

Rich DeVos, owner of the Orlando Magic and co-founder of Alticor, is a cheerleader par excellence. In an inspiring biography about Rich, Pat Williams quotes Rick Fiddler.

*On September 14, 1983, I was a young pilot in my late twenties, flying a Sikorsky S76 helicopter from Chicago to Grand Rapids with four Amway executives aboard. We had a problem with the tail rotor and ended up crashing into Lake Michigan. It was near sunset, and we were floating in life jackets in fifty-four-degree water. After about an hour, the Coast Guard picked us up and took us to the Chicago station.*

*While all this was going on, Rich was in his Florida home getting ready for dinner when he got a call informing him of the crash. Rich called the Coast Guard to find out about us and insisted on staying on the line until we were safe. When we got to the station in Chicago, someone told me, "There's a phone call for you—the man has been on hold for an hour, waiting for you."*

*I took the call, and it was Rich. He said he had been praying for us, and he was relieved that we were safe. The next day he flew back to Michigan. I was at the hangar when a call came in saying, "Mr. DeVos wants a helicopter ride. Pick him up in front of the company headquarters." I was still shaky from the crash, but I climbed into the company's other helicopter and took off. When I got to the headquarters, Rich was waiting for me. I let him in and said, "Where do you want to go?" He said, "I don't care. Let's just go for a ride."*[3]

> *Self-confidence energizes, and it gives your people the courage to stretch, take risks, and achieve beyond their dreams. It is the fuel of winning teams.*
>
> —JACK WELCH

I ask myself if I would have been that gracious. Would I be that committed to build confidence in a teammate? That day, the cheerleading of Rich DeVos built a lasting *self-confidence* in Rick Fiddler, a member of his team.

## Building Hope

Hope is expectation reaching into the future. It's directing your life toward a vision that is vitally important. It is energized by a Life Dream. Hope keeps you going in the dark because you believe the dawn is coming.

You build hope in your team members when you help them determine their Life Dream, coach them to look honestly where they are failing, encourage their solutions, and keep the potential of their dreams constantly in their vision.

Sometimes your biggest dreams don't turn out the way you want. King David knew that experience very well. One time he said his soul was "cast down," meaning that there was nothing he could do to right himself. He dialogs with his soul.

*Why are you cast down, O my soul,*
*and why are you in turmoil within me?*
*Hope in God; for I shall again praise*
*Him, my salvation and my God.⁴*

## Building Relationships

A third way to cheer the members of your team is to build up the relationships you have with them. Your strength as a leader depends to a great degree on the strength of the relationships you have built. Max De Pree, the former CEO of Herman Miller and author of highly acclaimed books on leadership, describes the connection between a leader and team.

> *Whether formally or informally, it's important to recognize that practically everything we accomplish happens through teamwork. We are not on our own. Everyone works within a loop of social accountabilities—a family, a congregation, a business. Ours is an arm-in-arm accountability.⁵*

In *The Art of Talking So That People Will Listen,*⁶ my co-author, Paul Swets, describes ten commitments that build "arm-in-arm accountability."

1. *I will be a friend.*
   If you want to have friends, even at work, you have to be a friend. Think about all the qualities you would want in a friend. List them on paper. Ask yourself which of those qualities you need to work on. Then commit yourself to improving those qualities with the members of your team.

2. *I will make the satisfaction, security, and development of my team as significant to me as my own.*
   This commitment has dynamite power in destroying barriers to trust and it has creative power in building strength into your relationships. Because of a natural inclination to self-focus, it is

not easy. But it represents the essence of what it means to "love your neighbor as yourself."

3. *I will make time for relationship building.*
   It is possible to be so dream driven that we neglect to cultivate the means by which our dreams are fulfilled. This is often true relative to our primary team, our own family. One study shows that married couples spend, on the average, only twenty-seven minutes out of every twenty-four hours talking with each other, but more than six hours per day watching TV. Strong relationships require the investment of time.

4. *I will celebrate the uniqueness of my teammate.*
   This commitment is counter-intuitive. We tend to want team members to be our clones—to think and act and feel just like we do. But a true arm-in-arm accountability is marked by freedom and respect for differences.

5. *I will avoid criticizing, condemning, and judging my team members.*
   This attitude is sensible and necessary because none of us is perfect. The "law of mutual exchange" is clear: if you judge others, you too will be judged. An attitude of personal support provides the best climate for positive change.

6. *I will initiate compliments.*
   Cycles of mutual retaliation often develop naturally. The "mutual exchange principle" here proceeds like this: "If you hurt my feelings, I'll hurt yours. If you say mean things to me, I'll say them back to you." But in healthy relationships, this cycle is pre-empted by the leader who initiates genuine compliments. For example:
   *I like the way you think.*
   *I respect you for making that tough telephone call.*
   *Your closing sentences were passionate and effective.*
   *You are doing the right things. Keep going. It's going to pay off.*

*You are a true friend. I enjoy being with you.*
*You are making a difference in people's lives.*
*Well done!*

7. *I will listen for and respond to feelings as well as thoughts.*
Clinical experience shows that when feelings are recognized
without judgment, they can be powerful motivating factors
for change. For example, if your team member has a
complaint, and you acknowledge that you understand the
complaint—and the feeling behind the complaint—you are
better able to coach her toward a solution.

8. *I will seek not so much to be understood as to understand.*
To *understand* means to stand on the same "ground" where
the other person is standing. It means to "walk in the other
person's shoes," to see reality through his or her eyes. We
can never understand another perfectly because reality
is always perceived by our own unique framework for
making sense of it. But we can come close. When we see a
frustration or joy from the other's viewpoint, as well as our
own, we increase the motivation for him to understand us.

9. *I will fight against the barriers to a healthy relationship.*
When most conflicts occur, the pattern is familiar: the
colliding of two opinions, the explosion of hostile words,
the psychological distance, the hurt feelings. You can change
that pattern by establishing four standards for your team.
   a. Avoiding yelling, insults, lies, deceit, name-calling, and
      bringing up past mistakes.
   b. Reflecting the other's feelings about a point, *to that*
      *person's satisfaction,* before arguing one's own point.
   c. Working through a disagreement with the goal of
      understanding and building the relationship—not
      winning the argument.
   d. Admitting when you're wrong.

10. *I will ask the greatest healing question.*
    When there is a break or strain in a relationship with a team member, there is one question that produces remarkable healing in relationships: *Will you forgive me for my contribution to the problem?* When you ask the question, you are not assuming all the blame for a problem. But you are acknowledging you contributed to it *to some degree*— which is likely true. Don't get bogged down in trying to determine who is most to blame. It's dead end. When the question is asked in all sincerity, mountains of bitterness can melt in a moment.

Arm-in-arm teamwork built on these ten commitments produces deep satisfaction. The cumulative effect of strong relationships is profound, always building a greater confidence, a vital hope, and the readiness of team members to encourage one another to pursue their individual and team dreams.

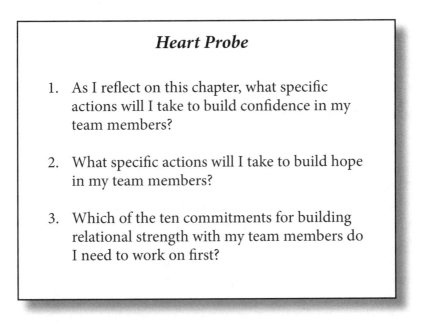

### *Heart Probe*

1. As I reflect on this chapter, what specific actions will I take to build confidence in my team members?

2. What specific actions will I take to build hope in my team members?

3. Which of the ten commitments for building relational strength with my team members do I need to work on first?

# Day 31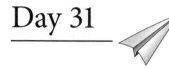

# Winning

*Your role as a leader is even more
important than you might imagine.
You have the power to help people become winners.*
—Ken Blanchard

## Overview

- *Winning Personally*
- *Winning with Your Team*
- *Winning Nationally and Internationally*
- *Winning the Crown*

### How do you intend to win in life?

In his book, *Winning,* Jack Welch asserts that an effective corporate mission statement basically answers one question: "How do we intend to win in this business?"[1] Building your Life Dream certainly includes a business dimension, but we have focused in these thirty-one days on a larger question: *"How do we intend to win in life?"* Your Life Dream impacts your whole life.

Winning in the pursuit of your dreams is one of the best things you can do. If you have developed your dreams wisely and if they energize your whole life, the implications are huge. In fact, how you win in life, how your Life Dream impacts your role as a leader may be *more important than you can imagine.* As a leader of a team, *you have in fact the power to help others become winners.*

Of course, it starts with you.

## Winning Personally

Winning implies struggle, overcoming opposing forces. Winning in the pursuit of your Life Dream, and helping other people become winners, is not easy. It's not for the timid. It's not for the self-centered. It's not for those who refuse to take the steps necessary to change and grow and become strong. Winning in the pursuit of your Life Dream assumes the need to train hard, think hard, and act with strength.

> *Winning a game lasts a moment. Winning at life lasts forever.*
>
> —Coach Tony Dungy, NFL Indianapolis Colts

No matter how strong you are, if you go after something of great value, you will likely fail time and again. Welcome failure because it will train you to be better. Embrace competition because it will force you to develop greater skill. Carefully consider criticism because it can give you valuable insight and inform you of things you may not have thought of. Winning personally is simply getting up and trying again when you fall. Are you tough enough to get up again, get stronger, and live like a champion?

We want you to win personally because here's what we know to be true. When you win in the pursuit of your dreams, you likely will

- grow in your personal development as a person
- feel upbeat about your future
- become the full time mother or father to your children if that is your desire
- not think about money all the time or how you will pay bills
- expand the horizons of your worldview and enrich the lives of others
- feel energized to do what matters most to you
- view each new day as a gift.

## Winning With Your Team

One of the themes we have considered throughout this book is that your Life Dream will enrich not only your life, but the lives of others as well, especially your team members—those partners who live and work and dream with you.

Walt Disney said there are three kinds of people in the world today.

- *Well poisoners*—people who discourage you and stomp on your creativity, and tell you what you can't do.
- *Lawn mowers*—people who tend to their own needs, mow their own lawns and never leave their yards to help another person.
- *Life enrichers*—people who reach out to enrich the lives of others, to lift them up and inspire them. Disney wanted to be a life enricher and surround himself with life enrichers.[2]

Your success can enrich your team. When one of your dreams is visibly successful, you gain credibility. Your team will trust you more as you teach them to dream. Until you have a dream that actually comes true, people find it difficult to trust your judgment on what will and will not work. But once you have a successful program, there is a turning point in their ability to trust your judgment.

When I saw the solid success of my mentors, it moved me beyond questioning my own judgment and wondering "Is this right? Can I do it? Will it work?" I used their success to build my confidence. Eventually my success made me more credible. Winning will do that for you as well. Your team will see the principles and activities that worked for you. Your winning encourages your team.

## Winning Nationally and Internationally

What will winning in pursuit of your Life Dream mean on a larger scale? If you are like most people, you may be thinking there is nothing you can do to make a positive contribution on a national or even international scale. That's not on your radar screen. It's not something you dream about. If that represents you, please think with us for a moment.

The great need today is for persons of good will to influence the world. There is a desperate need for persons of vision to transform culture. The world is in trouble and it needs your help.

It's true—it's easier to live quietly within the confines of your neighborhood; to "mow your own lawn;" to follow limited dreams; to wash your hands of the world and enjoy a few safe friends; to stifle national and international ambitions; to define yourself by your community rather than as a citizen of the world.

But suppose you have followed the steps outlined in this book for developing your Life Dream. Suppose you successfully enrich your life and many others as well. What if each team member catches your vision and develops their own Life Dream? What difference could even one person make whose life has been dramatically transformed by your influence? Are you dreaming big?

You do live in a very complex and needy world. But though you can't do everything to improve your world, will you refuse to do the few things within your power? Can you improve your leadership style in listening, encouraging and winning in ways that others will model and duplicate? Can you befriend a protégé, perhaps an international student, and pour into that person what you have been privileged to learn? Can you contribute time or money or your very self to some of the global concerns of our time? Could you support a medical mission effort, or a crisis relief agency, or the global efforts to combat hunger, AIDS, malaria, and hundreds of preventable diseases? Can you help your team to take on a cause? Do you realize that we can banish extreme poverty in our generation—yet eight million people die each year because they are too poor to survive?[3]

---

**DREAMING BIG**

*My dream is to make sad people happy, to give poor people hope, and to tell all people about God.*
—RUSSELL MTHEMBU
LADYSMITH BLACK MOMBAZZO
SOUTH AFRICA

---

We can ignore the brutal facts of our world or we can change the world—one person at a time. We encourage you not to be fearful or timid when you face the bullies with small minds or the giants of overwhelming need. Why not aim for the redemption of entire cultures as well as individuals? Let's dream big!

## Winning the Crown

One of the great debates in our culture involves the question of whether there is such a thing as Intelligent Design. In other words, is the present universe—cosmic and atomic, animate and inanimate—a product of design or mere chance? What difference does it make?

Some scientists are concerned that if they admit there is evidence of design, logic suggests they also will have to admit a designer of some sort. That scares them. Yet cosmologist Fred Hoyle wrote, "A super intellect has monkeyed with physics, as well as with chemistry and biology."[4]

In *The Cosmic Blueprint*, Paul Davies concluded, "The laws [of physics] . . . seem themselves to be the product of exceedingly ingenious design. [There] is for me powerful evidence that there is something going on behind it all . . . It seems as though somebody has fine-tuned nature's numbers to make the Universe . . . The impression of design is overwhelming."[5]

Obviously, blind chance scientists also have their reasons for their views. But think about this for a minute: What if there *is* a Designer and what if this Designer has a design for life? What are the implications?

What if each soul is immortal and that helping to change the trajectory of even one soul is a matter of infinite consequence? Do we really have the option of declining to become a world player?

> *The most important thing about a man is what he thinks about God.*
> —G. K. CHESTERSON

This type of world-and-life winning energized the Apostle Paul. He said,

"Forgetting what is behind and straining toward what is ahead, I press on toward the goal to win the prize. . . ."[6]

What is the winning goal for you? When you reach the end of your life, what will be the prize you have won? What life-changing legacy will you leave to your family, your children, your friends, your teammates?

*I have fought the good fight, I have finished the race, I have kept the faith. Now there is in store for me the crown . . .*[7]
—THE APOSTLE PAUL

Are you dreaming big? Are you encouraging big dreamers?

*Dream Big* • *Grow Personally* • *Change Your World*

---

### *Heart Probe*

1. As I finish reading *Dreaming Big*, what dreams are on my heart right now?

2. What is my plan to keep on dreaming big?

3. What actions will I take now to pursue my Life Dream?

---

S.D.G.

# Notes

## DAY 1

1. Victor Frankl, *Man's Search for Meaning* (Boston: Beacon Hill Press, 1959), 11.

## DAY 2

1. See Ecclesiastes 3:4.

## DAY 4

1. Used by permission from Masterplanning Group.
2. John R. Schneider, *The Good of Affluence* (Grand Rapids: William B. Eerdmans Publishing Company), 2002.

## DAY 5

1. Joseph Epstein, quoted in Hugh Hewitt, *In, But Not Of* (Nashville: Thomas Nelson Publishers, 2003), 1.

## DAY 8

1. See Psalm 25:4 NLT
2. Quoted in Stephen Covey, *The 8th Habit* (New York: Simon & Schuster, 2005), 42.

## DAY 9

1. Jim Collins, *Good to Great* (New York: Harper Collins, 2001), 1.

## DAY 10

1. Robert T. Kiyosaki, *Rich Dad, Poor Dad* (New York: Warner Books), 2000.
2. Kiyosaki, quoted from a taped interview entitled, "The Perfect Business."
3. If you are considering a career change, you may want to read a book that will help you think through the pros and cons of your decision. We have found Robert Kiyosaki's book helpful, *Before You Quit Your Job* (New York: Warner Business Books), 2005.

## DAY 11

1. Jack Welch, *Winning* (New York: Harper Collins Publishers), 2005.

## DAY 12

1. Pat Williams, *How to Be Like Rich DeVos* (Deerfield Beach, FL: Health Communications, 2004), 151.

## DAY 13

1. See Matthew 16:26.
2. Shelley Baur, *Commercial Appeal,* 9/12/03, C1.
3. Adapted from *Life @ Work Journal* (November / December 2000, Volume 3, Number 4), 80.
4. Pat Williams, *How to Be Like Rich DeVos,* 234.
5. Dietrich Bonhoeffer, *Cost of Discipleship* (New York: Simon & Schuster, 1995), 282.
6. Williams, Ibid.
7. Norman Cousins, *Human Options* (New York: W.W. Norton & Company, 1981), 68.
8. Sanders L. Willson, Baccalaureate Service at Second Presbyterian Church, May 10, 2006.

## DAY 14

1. Quoted in Rich DeVos, *Compassionate Capitalism* (New York: Dutton, 1993), 19.
2. Hugh Hewitt, *In, Not Of* (Nashville: Thomas Nelson Publishers, 2003), 19.
3. See Psalm 139:14.

## DAY 15

1. Special thanks to Derrick Johnson for sharing the story of the Wright brothers.
2. See Proverbs 1:7.
3. Martin Luther King, Jr. quoted in *We Shall Overcome: Martin Luther King, Jr. and The Black Freedom Struggle, edited by Peter J. Albert and Ronald Hoffman* (Pantheon Books in cooperation with the United States Capitol Historical Society, 1990).

## DAY 16

1. Dexter R. Yager Sr., *Don't Let Anybody Steal Your Dream* (Charlotte, North Carolina: Internet Services Corporation, 1978), 12.

## DAY 17

1. See Psalm 23:2 NLT.
2. See Romans 12:2.
3. See Psalm 42:11.
4. Phillip Keller, *A Shepherd Looks At Psalm 23* (Grand Rapids: Zondervan, 1970) 61.
5. Larry Crabb, *Shattered Dreams* (WaterBrook Press, 2002), 7.

## DAY 18

1. Paul Tournier, *The Strong and The Weak* (Philadelphia: The Westminster Press, 1963), 129.

## DAY 19

1. See 1 Chronicles 4:10.
2. See 1 Chronicles 4:10.

## DAY 20

1. Larry Crabb, *Shattered Dreams* (WaterBrook Press, 2002), 1.
2. Bobb Biehl, *Why You Do What You Do* (Nashville: Thomas Nelson Inc., 1993).

## DAY 21

1. Jeff Myers, *Handoff* (Dayton, TN: Passing the Baton International, 2006), 2.
2. See Bobb Biehl, *Mentoring* (Lake Mary, FL: Aylen Publishing), 2004.

## DAY 22

1. Max De Pree, *Leadership is an Art* (New York: Doubleday, 1989), 136.
2. Martin Luther King, Jr., *"I Have A Dream."* Delivered on the steps at the Lincoln Memorial in Washington D.C. on August 28, 1963.
3. See Luke 22:26.
4. See Luke 22:27.
5. Victor Frankl, *Man's Search for Meaning* (Boston: Beacon Hill Press), 1959.

## DAY 23

1. Ken Blanchard, *The Heart of a Leader* (Tulsa: Honor Books), 1999.

2.  John Wooden with Steve Jamison, *Wooden* (Chicago: Contemporary Books, 1997), 63.
3.  Pat Riley, *The Winner Within* (New York: The Berkley Publishing Group), 1963.
4.  Warren Bennis quoted in *Fortune*, September 19, 1994, 241.
5.  Bobb Biehl & Ted Engstrom, *Boardroom Confidence* (Lake Mary, FL: Quick Wisdom Publishing), 2001.

**DAY 25**

1.  Laurie Beth Jones, *Teach Your Team to Fish* (New York: Three Rivers Press), 2002.

**DAY 26**

1.  Quoted in Dexter R. Yager Sr., *Don't Let Anybody Steal Your Dream* (Charlotte, North Carolina: Internet Services Corporation), 1978.
2.  Bono, quoted in *Time*, November 7, 2005, 134.
3.  Norman Cousins, *Human Options* (New York: W.W. Norton & Company, 1981), 51.
4.  Pam Winters quoted from a speech on a CD entitled, *"Where We're Going,"* Disc 2, Track 2.

**DAY 27**

1.  John Crowe quoted from a speech on a CD entitled, *"Two Windows."*
2.  See David's confession in Psalm 51.

**DAY 29**

1.  Paul Swets, *The Art of Talking So That People Will Listen* (New York: Simon & Schuster), 1992. Adapted from chapter four.

**DAY 30**

1.  Pat Williams, *How to Be Like Rich DeVos* (Deerfield Beach, FL: Health Communications), 2004.
2.  Bob Burg, *Winning Without Intimidation* (Mechanicsburg, PA: Executive Books, 2005), 84.
3.  Williams, *How to Be Like Rich DeVos,* 107-8.
4.  See Psalm 42:5–6 ESV.
5.  Max De Pree, *Leadership Jazz* (New York: Dell Publishing, 1992), 22.

6. Paul Swets, *The Art of Talking So That People Will Listen* (New York: Simon & Schuster, 1992), 131.

**DAY 31**
1. Jack Welch, *Winning* (New York: Harper Collins, 2005), 14.
2. Pat Williams, *How to Be Like Rich DeVos*, 103.
3. *Time,* March 14, 2005, 44–45.
4. Fred Hoyle, *Home is Where the Wind Blows* (Sausalito, California: University Science Books, 1994), 16.
5. Paul Davies, *The Cosmic Blueprint* (Conshohocken, PA: The Templeton Foundation Press, 2004), 203.
6. See Philippians 3:13–14.
7. See 2 Timothy 4:7–8.

# Acknowledgments

For Paul and me, this project has been a big dream come true, and as you know . . . a big dream requires a team of people to succeed. This book is proof.

We are deeply indebted to the following members of our team for their diligent reading of the manuscript and wise comments: Professor Justin Barnard; Karen Brunsting; Marcia Buck; Jack Connors; Faith Curtis; Professor Bill Dwyer; Brett Easley; Bruce Harrington; Professor John Hodges; Sara Hazlip; Ethel Swets, Mary Teasley; and Karen Watson.

Our debt of gratitude has been greatly increased through our association with the Authentic Publishing staff—Volney James, Angela Lewis, Dana Carrington, and Paul Lewis. Janiece Swets supplied diligent and insightful editing. Without this team's applied wisdom and eager dedication to the task, this big dream would not have become a reality.

Team, every one of you is a winner. Thank you for your willingness to serve so enthusiastically and to cheer us on. We love you all!

# Helping You Win

Additional field-tested resources
can be ordered from www.Aylen.com

## *The Art of Talking So That People Will Listen*
by Paul Swets
*Over 100,000 copies sold*

Talking comes naturally, but getting people to really listen is another matter. It is an art and a skill and knowing how to get past the common barriers to understanding. In this very popular and helpful book, Dr. Paul Swets draws upon his doctoral research and counseling experience to assist us in dramatically increasing our ability to get through to people. It is an art most essential to our enjoyment of other people and the achievement of personal success. Dr. Norman Vincent Peale comments in the Foreword: "I wish that I might have had access to this book as a young man. In that case my proficiency in the art of communication would have been greatly enhanced. *The Art of Talking So That People Will Listen* is a masterpiece . . ."

## *Asking To Win!*
*Helpful 24 x 7 x 365 x life!*

This booklet fits into your suit coat pocket, purse, or briefcase. It contains over one hundred profound questions to help you make wise decisions twenty-four hours a day, seven days a week, for the rest of your life. Would you benefit from knowing how to ask penetrating, powerful, practical questions? Would you like to be able to ask exactly the "right questions" at the "right time"? This booklet works.

## *Career Change/LifeWork*
*30 Questions to Ask Before Making Any Major Career Change*

Is your current position "just a job," your next "career move," or your "lifework"?

This series of thirty questions comes in handy any time you are thinking about the possibility of making a work change. If you are uncertain, these profoundly simple ideas can help. You can also help friends in transition. You hand them the thirty questions; they may take hours to answer the questions, but they will come back with well-thought-out answers. These questions save hours of time in decision making.

Helpful in any career re-evaluating process between the ages of twenty-five to sixty. A proven resource!


## *The Effective Board Member*
by Bobb Biehl and Ted W. Engstrom

This one book turns boardroom anxiety, confusion, and frustration into . . . BOARDROOM CONFIDENCE!

Have you ever wished you could sit down and chat with a mentor who would help you be more confident and effective in your position on the board?

In *The Effective Board Member*, you now have available two seasoned boardroom veterans (with combined experience with over one hundred boards), eager to help you! This book is extremely helpful if you:

- Are trying to choose the right board members
- Serve on a board
- Need to make board presentations
- Are trying to decide whether to accept a board position
- Are new to a board
- Have been a board member a long while, but have never had any formal board training

Quantity discounts available so each member of your board can have her or his own copy.

## *Event Planning Checklist*
by Ed Trenner

This comprehensive THREE-HUNDRED-POINT CHECK LIST can cut your planning time in half, especially if you are new to "special events."

This checklist is designed for those who receive great pleasure from precision and for those who have yet to experience it. The three-hundred-point check list helps you keep from overlooking an obvious question and finding "egg-on-your-face" at the event. Practical, proven, easy-to-use.

## *Focusing By Asking*
Drive time CD

Profound questions have helped thousands of people, in all walks of life, at all levels of leadership, focus their lives and teams. This drive-time series is set up with five-minute tracks, covering the following ten critical elements of leadership:

**PERSONAL FOCUS –**
    Keeping FOCUSED
    Keeping CONFIDENT
    Keeping BALANCED
    Keeping MOTIVATED
    Keeping ORGANIZED

**TEAM FOCUS –**
    Master ASKING
    Master COMMUNICATING
    Master LEADING
    Master MOTIVATING
    Master PLANNING

Whenever you need to see things in crystal-clear focus, remember to pop in this drive-time CD or cassette tape.

## LEADING with Confidence

Approximately four thousand people have completed the (30 Days to) Confident Leadership (formerly titled Leadership Confidence) series. A wise, proven investment in your own future, this series is a life-long leadership reference covering thirty essential leadership areas, including:

- HOW TO COPE WITH—Change, Depression, Failure, Fatigue, Pressure
- HOW TO BECOME MORE—Attractive, Balanced, Confident, Creative, Disciplined, Motivated
- HOW TO DEVELOP SKILLS IN—Asking, Dreaming, Goal Setting, Prioritizing, Risk Taking, Influencing, Money Managing, Personal Organization, Problem Solving, Decision Making, Communicating
- HOW TO BECOME MORE EFFECTIVE IN—Delegating, Firing, Reporting, Team Building, People Building, Recruiting, Masterplanning, Motivating

## Masterplanning–Arrow

Masterplanning Arrow (24" x 36") helps you and your team quickly see:

THE "BIG PICTURE" . . . when you are drowning in detail
THE "FOREST" . . . when you feel lost in the trees
THE "SYMPHONY" . . . not just a few notes

The Masterplanning Arrow teaches you how to quickly sort out the direction of any organization, division, department, or major project you ever lead anywhere, at any time, for the rest of your life. The Arrow is now available with easy to follow step-by-step instructions on the back, even if you do not order the book or tape series.

## *Masterplanning–Book*

This series presents the same track the Masterplanning Group has refined in day-to-day consulting practice for over twenty-five years to help clients develop their Masterplans.

### The Process Has Been Used Successfully:
- From mom and pop organizations to a staff of thousands
- From start-up budgets to hundreds of millions a year
- From local churches to international organizations in over one hundred countries
- From small local churches (fifty) to large area churches (four thousand or more)
- From those with no business experience to Harvard MBAs

### Predictable Symptoms without a Masterplan

A Masterplan can be likened to a musical score for a symphony orchestra. "Unless everyone's on the same sheet of music, the result will not be pleasant to the ears." Without a Masterplan, expect the following:
1. DIRECTIONAL COMMUNICATIONS (internal and external) are foggy.
2. FRUSTRATION, TENSION, and PRESSURE develop because of differing assumptions.
3. DECISION MAKING is POSTPONED because a FRAMEWORK is not available for clear decisions.
4. ENERGY and RESOURCES ARE WASTED because the basic systems are not clearly developed.
5. FUNDING is INADEQUATE because of a lack of consistent communication to the organization's constituency.
6. The ORGANIZATION SUFFERS because the creative energies are spent putting out fires.

It is helpful to have a clear Masterplan.

## *Mentoring*
How to Find a Mentor and How to Become One

A mentoring relationship can easily add a feeling of 30 to 50 percent extra LIFE-LEADERSHIP HORSEPOWER to any person. Without a mentor, a person often feels underpowered, as if not living up to her or his true potential.

This powerful resource gives you very useful steps about forming a mentoring relationship and answers practical mentoring questions with proven answers.


## *Mid-life Storm*
Avoiding a "Mid-Life Crisis"

This hope-filled book contains a crystal-clear "Mid-Life Map," which helps guide you or a friend successfully through the very dangerous mid-life years.

Just because you or your mate is beginning to ask a few mid-life questions does not automatically mean you are experiencing the dreaded "Mid-Life Crisis." There are three distinctly different mid-life phases:
- Mid-Life Re-evaluation
- Mid-Life Crisis
- Mid-Life Drop Out

This book addresses each of the three phases with specific step-by-step instructions on how to avoid the pain and confusion of a mid-life crisis—or if you are already there, how to get out and get on with the rest of your life.

## On My Own
An ideal graduation gift!

Many adults have said that they wish their parents had taught them these principles before they started off "on their own." Parents, as well as students, benefit from these extremely fundamental leadership principles.

If you have been increasingly concerned about your high school or college student's readiness to face the "real world," this book has been written for your son or daughter.

These principles will stay with your son or daughter for a lifetime. And they can pass them on to their children's children.

## Pre-Marriage: Getting To "Really Know" Your Life Mate-To-Be
*Pre-marriage Questions*

These are the heart-to-heart questions you ask before you say "I Do" to make sure this is the right person for you. It is hard to break up any relationship, but it is far better to break an engagement than a marriage. Most couples find that they have far more in common than they had even realized. The handful of major disagreements can be discussed before marriage to see if they are major differences which are "engagement breakers" or if they are just uncomfortable differences.

If you have any doubts at all about your upcoming marriage—and just want to make sure this is the life mate for you—this book can help! A very appropriate pre-marriage gift for any friend.

## Stop Setting Goals

Do you hate setting goals—or know someone who does?

Then this book is for you! The most common reaction to this book is: "I no longer feel like a second-class citizen!" This simple paradigm shift has already freed thousands of readers for life!

As a team leader, you can reduce team tensions and, at the same time, significantly increase team spirit by introducing this simple idea at your next staff meeting.

## Strategy Work Sheets
*(11" x 17")*

A quick, systematic, step-by-step method to think through a solid success strategy for each of your goals. Use these sheets to ask each staff member to draft a strategy for turning each major goal into a realistic plan. *Strategy Work Sheets* help you spot problems in basic thinking and strategy before those problems become costly. Includes twenty-four sheets for use with your team.

## Team Profile
*"What makes you tick?" "What turns you on?" "What burns you out?"*

The *Team Profile* is a proven (7th edition—18th printing since 1980) way of understanding yourself better. In simple language, it lets you tell your spouse, your friends, or your colleagues what makes you "tick." *Team Profile* clarifies what you really want to do, not what you have to do, have done the most, or think others expect of you. It is the key to understanding personal fulfillment and is an affordable way of building strong team unity by predicting team chemistry. This profoundly simple, self-scoring, self-interpreting inventory is the key to selecting the right person for the right position, thus helping avoid costly hiring mistakes.

## *Why You Do What You Do*
4th Printing

This book is a result of over forty thousand hours of behind-the-defenses experiences with some of the finest, emotionally healthy leaders of our generation. This model was developed to maximize "healthy" people with a few emotional "mysteries" still unanswered!

Why do I have a phobic fear of failure, rejection, or insignificance? Why am I so "driven" to be admired, recognized, appreciated, secure, respected, or accepted? Why am I an enabler, leader, promoter, rescuer, controller, people pleaser? Why am I a perfectionist, workaholic? Why are pastors vulnerable to affairs? Where am I the most vulnerable to temptation? How do I guard against temptation? Why do I have such a hard time relating to my parents when I love them so much? Why do they sometimes seem like such children?

These and other "emotional mysteries" can be understood and resolved in the silence of your own heart without years of therapy.


## *Writing Your First Book!*
Bobb Biehl and Mary Beshear, Ph.D.

If you have been wanting to write a book for years, but still haven't finished a manuscript, let *Writing Your First Book!* be your starting point! This is a skeleton outline—no complicated, sophisticated theory, or double talk. It is just a bare bones, easy-to-follow, step-by-step checklist to become a royalty-receiving author. A wise investment in your own future.

# QuickWisdom.com

## AN INTRODUCTION . . . AND AN INVITATION!

As an executive mentor/consultant, I have the rare privilege of spending days at a time with some of the finest leaders of our generation. I continue to grow personally, learning more in the past year than I've learned in the five years before it.

## Mentoring Realities

In my book *Mentoring*, I define mentoring ideally as "a lifelong relationship in which the mentor helps the protege grow into her/his God-given potential over a lifetime." Realistically, because of schedule pressures, my personal mentoring is limited to a very few individuals. At the same time, I truly want to see friends like you grow into your God-given potential over your lifetime.

Solomon advised, "Get Wisdom."

The search of today seems to be focused on becoming a courageous, charming, powerful, successful person. However, according to the Bible, Solomon, who was one of the wisest, if not the wisest, man that ever lived, gave us this profound and timeless bit of advice in Proverbs 4:5 . . . GET WISDOM! This is advice that our modern world seems to overlook.

Enter the idea of **Quick Wisdom.**

The focus of **Quick Wisdom** is to help you and your friends be WISE!

Today, it seems to me that every young leader I meet wants wisdom, but needs it fast. We don't have the time with today's pace and pressures to go to a mountaintop and study ancient manuscripts in Sanskrit. Thus—"Quick Access to Timeless Wisdom." My focus: three to ten times times per month I plan to send "QuickWisdom" emails to pass on the very best "wisdom nuggets" I can give you each month to help strengthen you and your friends. Free to you and your friends.

**Quick Wisdom** is one hundred percent free to you and your friends.

Fortunately, the email technology of today is such that you can enroll ten friends or one-hundred to receive the **Quick Wisdom** email. It takes me the same amount of time to send you an email as it does to send it to all of your protégés/friends. I want to use my unique exposure to great wisdom to strengthen you and your friends for a lifetime.

Thank you, my friend, for telling your friends about **Quick Wisdom**!

**To sign up for Quick Wisdom, go to www.QuickWisdom.com.**

# Speaking Topics/Bobb Biehl

## *Personal Development*

### Focusing Your Life

- ❏ **"Fog Cutting Arrow"**
  *Clarifying Any Topic Quickly . . . Avoiding the Frustration of Mental Fog*
- ❏ **"The NorthStar"**
  *Keeping a Clear Sense of Life Direction . . . Avoiding the "Lost At Sea" Feeling*

### Asking "Fog-Cutting" Questions

- ❏ **"The Dream Sparking Questions"**
  *Getting Your Thinking "Outside of the Box" . . . Avoiding "Same ol' Same ol'" Results*

### Balancing Competing Priorities

- ❏ **"The Annual Balance Calendar"**
  *Balancing Your Life . . . Avoiding the Feeling of the Day to Day Busyness Drift*

### Communicating With Confidence

- ❏ **"The You Focus Model"**
  *Mastering "You Focus" . . . Avoiding "Egocentric" Communication*

## *Organizational Development*

### Planning Your Organization's Future

- ❏ **"The Team Focus Arrow" (50,000 Foot Level)**
  *Focusing Top Leadership's Thinking . . . Avoiding Team Confusion*
- ❏ **"The Masterplanning Arrow" (20,000 Foot Level)**
  *Getting Your Team on the "Same Sheet of Music" . . . Reducing Team Mis-Communication*
- ❏ **"The Boulders Sheet" (Organizational Level)**
  *Keeping Your Team Focused on Boulders . . . Avoiding Team Drift and Stagnation*

### Building A "Championship" Team

- ❏ **"The Leadership Star"**
  *Upgrading Your Current Team . . . Avoiding "Bureaucratic" Thinking*

### Generating Consistent Cash Flow
❏ **"The Marketing Process"**
*Generating Profit . . . Avoiding a "Warehouse Full of Unsold Inventory"*

### Managing Resources Wisely
❏ **"The 'Vital Signs' & 'Standards' of Healthy Growth"**
*Projecting Your Team's 10-Year Future . . . Avoiding Dangerous Trends (Blind Spots)*

Please send me the following (free of charge):
❏ Masterplanning Group's tool catalog
❏ Consulting information
❏ Speaking information

Name _____

Title _____

Organization _____

Address _____

City _____ State _____ Zip _____

Daytime telephone (_____) _____

Fax (_____) _____

E-Mail _____

### Contact:
**Fax:** (352) 385-2827
**Toll free fax:** (888) 443-1976
**Ordering:** (800) 443-1976
**Web:** www.Aylen.com